Dead Asleep

Jensen Beach Mysteries

Dead Asleep
Jensen Beach Mysteries

By

Rodney Riesel

Independently Prepared by Island Holiday Publishing
East Greenbush, NY

Special thanks to:

Pamela Guerriere

Kevin Cook

Cover Image by:

Andriy Popov

www.123rf.com/profile_andreypopov

Cover Design by:

Connie Fitsik

To learn about my other books friend me at

https://www.facebook.com/rodneyriesel

For Brenda,
Kayleigh, Ethan
& Peyton

Chapter One

John Burton and Kurt Powell sat in matching lounge chairs on the concrete decking around the inground pool John recently had installed. Two bottles of LandShark Lager sat on a table between the men, best friends since high school. It was another postcard-perfect day in the Treasure Coast town of Jensen Beach, Florida. Light traffic hummed along Indian River Drive. All was right with the world.

Kurt tipped his bottle up, guzzled, and swallowed. "This is the life," he said. "Eighty-five degrees, not a cloud in the sky … sitting by a pool, cold beer in hand."

John picked up his beer and clinked it against John's. "Cheers, pal."

"You got any cigars?"

"I don't think you should be smoking cigars." John took a swig of his beer.

"I think you're wrong. A cigar is just what I need."

"It's only been three weeks since your broken ribs and collapsed lung. You probably shouldn't be sucking smoke into that lung."

A few weeks earlier Kurt had been attacked in his own driveway by a group of men attempting to warn him and John off a case they were working on—the murder of Kimberly Levesque.

"I won't inhale the smoke."

"You're not getting a cigar."

"Whatever, M*om*." Kurt turned to look over his shoulder, at the house next door. He winced in pain, and grabbed his side.

"What are you looking for?" John asked.

"What do you think?"

"Cassie?"

"Yeah. I was hoping she would come over more often now that you have a pool."

"She was here last night."

"Are ya shittin' me! Why didn't you call me?"

"You want me to give you a call every time a woman is here swimming in my pool?"

"Just the hot ones. No need to tell me when there's an uggo here."

"An uggo," John repeated, shaking his head. "Don't expect any calls."

"How about if we set up a Bat-Signal, like Batman has. Only instead of a bat, the beacon could project a big set of boobs in the sky. We could call it the Boob-Signal."

"Sometimes I feel like we're having the same conversations we had when we were thirteen."

"Your point being?"

"I guess I don't have a point."

"Can we turn on some music?"

"The speakers aren't hooked up yet. The stereo guy is supposed to be back on Friday."

"When are they gonna start putting up the screened room?"

"Monday."

Kurt looked back over his shoulder at Cassie's house again. "She must know we're out here. Maybe you should give her a call and ask her to come over and have a beer with us."

"Why?"

"It's the neighborly thing to do."

"How often do you have *your* neighbors over?"

"Never. I don't have a pool, and if I did, I wouldn't want to see Old Lady Hamburg in a bathing suit. Come on, give her a call."

"I'm not giving her a call. Besides, I thought you were interested in Bonnie over at Mulligan's."

"I am, but she's turned me down like twenty-eight times now, dude. I'm starting to think no really does mean no."

"You're just starting to think that?"

The pain on Kurt's face was obvious when he sat up in his lounge chair. "Man, I didn't think these ribs would still hurt this bad."

"The doc said it takes awhile for ribs to heal."

Kurt stood. A dense constellation of freckles peppered his bony shoulders. His skinny, deathly pale legs stuck out of his board shorts like a pair of Q-tips.

"My God, you are a beanpole," John remarked. "If you turned sideways and stuck out your tongue, you'd look like a zipper.

"How original … *not*. I think I'll go back in the pool while you're getting me another beer."

"Feel free to go in and get your own beer."

"I'm hurt, dude. You better get it. I wouldn't be in this shape if it wasn't for you."

"Wasn't for me!" John shouted. "How do you figure?"

"This whole solving crime thing with you is what got me all busted up."

"But it was your idea! It's always your idea. I'm the one who says, 'Let the cops handle it,' but no, you want to play private dick."

Kurt grabbed his crotch. "I got your private dick right here. Now, go get me a beer." He turned and dove into the water.

John waited for his friend to resurface. When he did, he said, "Maybe you shouldn't be diving into the pool until you're all healed up."

Kurt hoisted himself up by his spaghetti-thin forearms on the pools coping, then shook the water out of his long, curly red hair like an Irish setter. "No cigars. No diving. No neighbor woman. No music. It's like a monastery over here."

John turned and walked into the house to grab a couple more beers. When he returned poolside, Kurt was back in his chair, rubbing his ribs.

"What's the matter?" John asked, handing his friend a beer.

"Maybe I shouldn't dive into the pool for a while," Kurt replied.

"Where have I heard that before? Oh yeah, I said it."

John twisted the top off his bottle and took a sip.

Cassie's back screen door squeaked open. Kurt's head spun around.

"Hey, Cassie!" Kurt hollered, raising his beer bottle in the air. "Can I get you a beer?"

"So, you can get *her* a beer," said John, "but I have to walk all the way in the house and get you *your* beers?"

"I'll be right over!" Cassie shouted back. She turned and went back inside.

"That's right, tiny dancer," Kurt whispered to himself, "you go put on that skimpy black bikini I like."

John chuckled. "You never cease to amaze me."

"Go get her a beer," Kurt said.

"You go get her a beer," John shot back.

Kurt groaned. "Sure, make the crippled guy do it." He climbed out of his lounge and walked slowly toward the back door, playing up his injury as he hobbled along.

As Kurt went through John's back door, Cassie exited hers. She wasn't wearing the skimpy black bikini. Instead, she was wearing a blue strapless bikini top and cut off denim shorts. Although the well-toned exotic dancer always looked gorgeous no matter what she wore—or *didn't* wear—John knew Kurt was going to be disappointed.

"Kurt sitting here?" Cassie asked, when she reached the concrete skirting.

"Yeah," John replied, "but sit down. He can drag one of the other ones over."

"Where'd he go?"

"Inside to get you a beer. He was hoping you'd be wearing that little black bikini you wore the last time he was here."

Cassie snickered. "He was, was he?"

"Also, he thinks I need to install a beacon in the shape of breasts to let him know when you're here. He wants to call it the Boob-Signal."

Cassie chuckled. "He's crazy."

The back door opened, and Kurt came out holding three bottles. Noticing Cassie was in his seat, his eyes went to one of the other lounge chairs.

"I don't think I'm going to be able to lift one of those lounge chairs," said Kurt. He handed Cassie one of the beers and set the other two on the table.

"I'll get it," John sighed.

When John walked back over with the lounge, he purposely placed it so he would be sitting between Kurt and Cassie. Making elaborate eye gestures that made him look like Marty Feldman having a seizure, Kurt tried to get John to move the lounge next to Cassie.

"What's the matter?" John asked.

"Nothing," Kurt replied.

"Why are you doing that with your eyes?"

"I'm not doing anything with my eyes."

Cassie looked back and forth from John to Kurt, wondering what was going on.

"Is the lounge good here?" John asked.

"It's fine."

"Oh, because I thought you were trying to get me to move it somewhere else," John said.

"No I wasn't."

"Are you sure?" John ribbed. "You were moving your eyes all around like you weren't happy with where I put it."

"Shut up, and sit down," Kurt said through his teeth.

"Wait. Did you want me to put the chair next to Cassie, Kurt? Did you want to sit next to Cassie? I can move it over next to Cassie."

"It's fine where it is," Kurt said angrily.

"So, you don't want to sit next to me?" Cassie asked, feigning disappointment. "Is it because I didn't where the black bikini?"

Kurt locked eyes with John. "What black bikini?" Kurt asked. "I don't know what you're talking about."

"I promise, the next time I wear the black bikini, I'll have John notify you with the Boob-Signal."

John and Cassie both burst out laughing.

"You guys are *sooo* funny," Kurt said. "You should take your show on the road." He snatched up one of the beers and took a seat on the lounge.

"I'm just bustin' your nads, string bean," Cassie assured him.

"Whatever."

"Working tonight?" John asked.

"Seven o'clock," Cassie replied. "You guys stopping over?"

"John's not allowed at the Doll House anymore," said Kurt. "Jessica put a stop to that."

"No she didn't. He's lying."

"She said she didn't want you over there."

"She said she didn't *like* it when I went over there."

"How'd she find out you were there?" Cassie asked.

"He told her," Kurt said.

"Most men don't mention to their wives or girlfriends when they go to a gentleman's club," Cassie said.

"He's a *true* gentleman," said Kurt.

"It's a new relationship," John defended. "I just thought it best not to start it off with lies."

"I admire honesty in guys," said Cassie. "However, Jessica used to be a dancer herself, so why would she have a problem with it?"

"Girlfriend's a stripper, neighbor's a stripper," Kurt grumbled. "Some guys have all the luck."

"My girlfriends not a stripper," John said. "She *used* to be a stripper."

"What's wrong with stripping?" Cassie asked. She tipped up her bottle.

"Nothing," John said. "I just wouldn't want my girlfriend doing it."

"Oh, wow."

Kurt piped in. "Uh, Cassie, just for the record, I would be perfectly fine if my girlfriend was a stripper."

Cassie smiled. "I'll keep that in mind, string bean."

Kurt nodded. "It's nice we already have pet names for each other."

John felt his cell phone vibrate. He reached into the pocket of his board shorts and took it out.

"Speak of the devil," John said. "Hey, Jessica."

"What's up?"

"Not much. Just sitting by the pool."

"Kurt there?"

"Kurt's here."

"Cassie there?"

"Cassie's here."

Cassie put on an over-animated grin when she heard her name mentioned.

"She wearing that black bikini?" Jessica asked.

"No, Jess."

"What's she wearing?"

"I can't say."

"Why can't you say?"

John turned his head away. "Because she's sitting right here," he whispered.

"Whatever."

"Is this why you called … to see who's here, and what they're wearing?"

"No, I just called to say hi. I'll let you go."

Jessica hung up the phone.

"Jess—dammit."

"She hang up on you?" Kurt asked.

"No," John lied.

"'Cause it sounded like she hung up on ya."

"She didn't."

"Your story."

"She mad because I'm here?" Cassie asked.

"Yup."

"I can go if ya want me to."

"No, don't be ridiculous," Kurt said. "You stay right where you are."

"Yeah, you don't have to leave," said John. "I don't know what her problem is."

"Is she like this with other women?" Cassie asked.

"Nope. Just you."

"What's there not to like about Cassie?" Kurt asked dreamily. He practically had throbbing hearts dancing around his still-dripping head, like a smitten cartoon character.

"She thinks she lost her job at the Doll House because of me," Cassie offered.

"Why would she think that?" Kurt asked.

"Because when I started at the Doll House, she was already working there. I was, like, twenty, and she was, like, thirty. After I was there for a few months, Russel started giving me the better shifts. Jessica started accusing me of sleeping with Russel—I wasn't. He's like five hundred pounds, for Chrissakes."

"That would probably crush you," Kurt pointed out.

"I'd just get on top," said Cassie.

Kurt's jaw dropped open.

"Then ya know what I'd do?" Cassie asked.

"What would you do?" Kurt said with a devilish grin.

"I wouldn't do anything, ya pervert. Like I said, he's five hundred pounds."

"That was very anticlimactic," said Kurt.

"Just like all your sexual encounters, real and imagined," said John. He turned to Cassie. "How long after you started did Jessica quit?"

"About six months, but it wasn't because of me. She was taking college courses at night for a long time. She always talked about getting out of the business. Finally, she did. I don't know why she blames me."

"Probably just her old lady ego," Kurt said.

"She's only forty-two," said John.

"I know, but compared to Cassie … I mean, come on."

"Wow, Kurt," John said.

"No offense," said Kurt.

"Oh, I know," John said sarcastically. "I can't imagine any woman would take offense to that."

"In a way," said Cassie, "I know how she feels. I'm thirty-one now, and this little bitch they just hired thinks she's the cat's shit. Tiny little thing. I hate her. All the regulars are going nuts over her. Perverts."

"What night does she work?" Kurt inquired. "Asking for a friend, of course."

"Of course."

"No, really. What nights?"

"You're scoring no points at all right now, string bean."

"I just wanted to show up when she was dancing, so I could boo her."

"I bet—oh, ya know what?"

"What?" said John.

"Speaking of work, there was something I was going to ask you."

"Let me guess," Kurt said. "The Doll House is looking for two male dancers, and you suggested John and me."

"Not even close."

"Then what could it be?"

"One of the girls—a waitress, not a dancer—was telling us this crazy story the other night."

"Story about what?" John asked.

"Well, believe it or not, Rosie—Rosie Barlow, that's my friend's name—said she had a dream that a woman was going to die."

"Okay."

"And about a week later, the woman did die."

"You're saying your friend Rosie predicted someone's death."

"Yes."

John stroked his cleft chin meditatively. "Which brings up the question, why didn't Rosie tell the woman?"

"Because she didn't know who the woman was."

"If Rosie didn't know who the woman was, then how does she know that the woman died?" Kurt asked.

"Because, when Rosie dreamed about her, she didn't get her name. She only knew a few things about her, but it was enough to recognize her when she read the woman's obituary a week later."

"What was the woman's name?" asked John.

"I don't remember."

"How did she die?"

"I don't remember what Rosie said. So, you guys think she's telling the truth?"

"Probably," said Kurt.

"No," said John, "she's not telling the truth."

"Why would she make up a story like that?"

"Yeah, John," said Kurt, "why would she make up a story like that?"

"Because she's a liar," John said.

"And you think all strippers are liars," Kurt surmised.

"No," said John. "I don't think all strippers are liars."

"Rosie's a waitress," Cassie reminded him. "Do you think all waitresses are liars?"

"No."

"Oh, wait," said Cassie, "I forgot to tell you the best part. Rosie had another dream on Monday night. There's a *guy* who's going to die this time."

"That's not really the best part of the story," John pointed out.

"Especially if the guy's gonna die," Kurt added.

"No one's going to die," said John.

"Someone's gonna die," said Kurt. "Heck, forty thousand men and women die every day."

Cassie looked puzzled. "Where'd you get that figure?"

"Duh! Blue Oyster Cult, of course. A little diddy called 'Don't Fear The Reaper.' Killer guitar riff."

"I'm not saying it," John assured his friend.

"Say it," Kurt prodded.

"Say what?" Cassie asked.

"Say it!" Kurt shouted.

"Needs more cowbell," John mumbled.

"What's that?" Kurt asked. "I didn't hear you."

"Needs more cowbell."

"There ya go."

Cassie just sat there bewildered. Part of her wanted to ask, but a bigger part didn't give a rat's ass what the two men were talking about. She wrote it off as, they're old, I'm young.

John waited for Kurt to finish his air guitar solo and then returned his attention to Cassie. "Kurt's right, Cassie," he said. "Death is a fact of life. When and if the guy dies, your waitress friend Rosie will lie and say she predicted it."

"Yeah," Cassie said angerly, "because all waitresses lie."

John sighed. "You're twisting my words, Cassie."

"Let's drop it, already! I just thought it was a pretty cool story."

"That's all it is, a story," John assured her.

Cassie smirked. "You know John, for somebody from Hollywood, you have zero imagination." She drummed her fingers on her golden legs a moment and added, "It's like a morgue around here. You got any music?"

"Speaker guy comes on Friday," said Kurt. "Screen enclosure guy comes on Monday."

Cassie hopped off the lounge. "I'll run home and grab my Bluetooth speaker." She sprinted across the yard. Kurt's lovesick gaze followed every jiggling step. "Shake that moneymaker, shake that moneymaker," he chanted, in a trance-like state.

John reached over and physically turned his soggy head around to face him.

"Give it up, pal," said John. "She's major league, and you're still playing tee-ball."

Kurt had to laugh. "Ya know what ya need out here?" he said.

"Less people?" John replied.

"A little fridge to keep beer in, so we don't have to keep running in the house."

Cassie returned to the pool and placed her small speaker on the table. She pulled out her phone. "What kind of music do you guys want to hear?" she asked.

"Zeppelin, Jefferson Airplane," said Kurt.

"The Who, the doors," John said.

"Anyone who's still alive?" Cassie asked.

"Most of them are still alive," Kurt shot back. He looked to John. "Right?"

John thought for a second. "I'm pretty sure more of them are alive than dead."

"Volunteers" by Jefferson Airplane began playing, and Cassie put her phone on the table next to the speaker.

"Love this song," Kurt stated.

"So did my grandfather," Cassie joked. She stood and walked to the edge of the pool and began wiggling out of the denim cut offs. When they dropped to her ankles, she used her toes to toss them aside. The thin backed bottoms didn't leave much to the imagination.

Cassie rose upon her tiptoes and dove into the water. She did the backstroke across the length of the pool, executed a flip turn and swam back, stopping midway. "Come on in, boys, the water's fine!" she called out, treading water. Her breasts bobbed in the water like two fleshy torpedoes. John and Kurt grinned idiotically and made identical no, we're fine gestures. "Suit yourself!" Cassie yelled, and took another lap.

"Are we supposed to stuff a fiver in her swimsuit?" Kurt asked. "I feel like we are."

"I don't know what you're talking about, Kurt," said John. "I didn't see anything."

Chapter Two

Friday morning Kurt pulled his turquoise 1973 Volkswagen van into John's driveway and shut off the engine. He jumped out of the old van and walked up to John's front door. He entered like he always did, without knocking.

"John!" Kurt shouted. He walked to the foot of the stairs and hollered again. "John!" There was still no answer.

Kurt lumbered through the living room, into the kitchen, and to the back door. He could see John standing at the far end of the pool near the small waterfall. Kurt opened the door and stepped onto the patio.

John glanced over when he heard the door shut. "Hey, Kurt," he said.

"You ready to go?" Kurt asked.

"Yeah, I'm ready. Just waiting for the stereo guy. He was supposed to be here at eight."

Kurt pulled out his cell phone and looked at the time—8:27.

"There's coffee in there," John offered. "Get yourself a cup."

Kurt went back into the kitchen and poured himself a mug of coffee. He brought it up to his nose and took a whiff. "M-mm—coconut."

John was seated in one of the lounge chairs when Kurt returned to the pool. He sat down in one of the other lounges.

Kurt blew into his coffee and tested it with his tongue. It was still too hot. He blew into it again. "Where are the speakers going?" he asked.

John pointed to the far end, near the waterfall. "There's four of them. Two down there will look like rocks." He pointed to the opposite end, near the hot tub. "The other two will be there. They're little round speakers on a three-foot pole."

"Pretty cool." Kurt sipped his coffee.

John's cell phone rang. "Hello? Okay … Yeah, that's fine." He hung up. "Let's go," he said, climbing out of his lounge chair.

"Who was that?" Kurt asked.

"Stereo guy. Something came up. He won't be able to make it until Monday."

"That's horse shit."

"Oh well, what're ya gonna do?"

Kurt stood. "Call him back and tell him that it's unacceptable. Tell him to get his ass over here and install those damn speakers. That's what I'd do."

"Would ya?"

"Probably not." Kurt shrugged. "I don't know. The guy who was supposed to paint the back of my store last year still hasn't showed up this year."

John walked through the house, locked his doors, and met Kurt in the driveway. They boarded the micro bus, and hit the road.

*****

Violet Jones was standing behind the bar staring at her cell phone when John and Kurt stepped up into the bar at Mulligan's Beach House Bar and Grill. She started to put her phone down when she caught sight of them.

"Oh, it's just you guys," she said, and brought the phone back up to her face.

"Just us guys?" Kurt aped. "You really know how to make a customer feel welcome."

"If I do," said Violet, "it's completely by accident."

John and Kurt sat down on their favorite barstools, with their backs to Indian River Drive.

"Bloody Mary, please," Kurt ordered.

"Just a cup of coffee for me," said John.

"Yeah, just a second," Violet said. "Let me finish this."

"Yeah, we're in no hurry," Kurt dead panned. "You just take your time."

When Violet had finally finished and sent the book-length text message she was writing, she tossed her cell phone on the back bar behind her.

"Bloody Mary," she said, pointing at Kurt.

"Yes."

Her finger swung over to John. "And a cup of coffee."

"Correct."

Violet poured John's coffee first and placed his mug in front of him, then she went to work on Kurt's Bloody Mary.

John cringed with the first sip of coffee. "Jesus," he said. "How long has this coffee been sitting there?"

Violet shrugged. "I don't know. It was there when I got here at six."

"You mean you didn't make it?"

"Nope."

"Has it been sitting there since last night?"

"John, I really doubt that pot of coffee has been sitting on that burner since last night."

John took a few more sips and then slid the cup back across the bar. "Can you make me a fresh pot?" he asked.

"Sure," said Violet. "Let's pour out a whole pot of coffee and make a fresh one for the movie star." She placed Kurt's Bloody Mary in front of him. "There ya go, Kurt. Let me know if that's not up to Hollywood standards."

Kurt snickered. "I sure will."

Violet picked up the mug and dumped it in the bar sink. "I suppose you want a new cup as well."

"Is something wrong?" John asked. "You're being a little mean to me today."

"Oh, no, John, nothing's wrong," Violet replied in that tone of voice that lets you know, yeah, something's wrong.

"What is it?" John asked.

"My mother said you had that stripper over to your house again."

Kurt was grinning big. He loved it when John was getting bitched at.

"Cassie's my neighbor," John defended. "That's all, nothing more. She comes over for a beer now and then. She comes over to swim. We're just friends."

"John, no one can be *just friends* with a stripper."

"Listen, Violet, I like your mom a lot. We have a lot of fun together, but she can't tell me who I can be friends with and who I can't."

Violet sighed. "I know. You're right. I've just never seen my mom like this. She really likes you, and I don't want to see her get hurt." Violet grabbed another mug off the back bar. "I'll run to the kitchen and get you a fresh cup."

After Violet left the room, John turned to his pal. "Hey, do you think Violet gave me yesterday's coffee on purpose?"

"Probably," said Kurt.

"If her mom and I ever break up, we'll never be able to come here again."

"That would be my guess."

"I like this place."

"Then don't screw up."

Violet returned with the coffee. "Here, this should be better."

John took a sip. "Much."

Violet gave them each a menu. She took their orders and returned to the kitchen.

"Speaking of Cassie," said Kurt, "what do ya think about that lady who dreams about people who are going to die?"

"I don't think anything about it," John answered.

"What if she's telling the truth?"

"She's not."

"How do you know?"

"Because I know."

"I've seen some pretty strange things, John."

"No you haven't."

"Oh, I have."

"Name one strange thing you've seen."

"This one time a ghost was—"

"Were you drinking?"

"Yeah."

"Name one strange thing you've seen when you weren't drinking."

"Okay, when my wife and I went to Key West this one time, she wanted to have her palm read."

"Why not green?"

"Ha! Funny. But seriously, we went to this guy on Flagler Avenue. His name was the Amazing Gary."

John shook his head. "The Amazing *Gary*? What's the matter, was the name the Amazing Delbert already taken?"

"Are ya gonna listen, or just make fun?"

"Probably a little of both. Go on."

"The guy predicted my wife and daughter's deaths."

"What? How's that possible? He actually told you your wife and daughter were going to die?"

"Well, not in so many words. The things he said were very cryptic, but later, after it happened, it all made sense."

"Yeah, Kurt, that's what all so-called psychics do—they prey on their victims' gullibility. They take advantage of the fact that people tend to accept generalizations that could be applied to anybody as uniquely applicable to them. The phenomenon is called the Barnum effect, after P.T. Barnum—the showman who coined the phrase, 'There's a sucker born every minute.' That guy you talked to in Key West didn't predict anything. No one can predict the future."

"What makes you so smart?" Kurt asked snidely.

"Well, uh … there was an episode of *Law of the Land* devoted to the subject."

"Oh yeah," Kurt recalled fondly. "'Land's End.' Great episode, but I still say there are some folks who can predict the future."

"Who's predicting the future?" Violet asked, as she stepped back behind the bar.

"No one," John replied.

"This woman that Cassie knows," said Kurt. "Some chick named Rosie."

"She can predict the future?"

"No," John said. "She can't."

Violet focused her attention on Kurt. "What did she predict?"

John rolled his eyes.

"Rosie had a dream awhile back that a woman was going to die," Kurt explained. "Then, a few days later, the woman was killed."

"No one said the woman was killed," John said.

"Oh my God!" said Violet, ignoring John's input. "That's crazy. Why didn't she warn the woman?"

"Because," Kurt said, "she didn't know the woman's name until after she died."

"Oh, I see," Violet said, nodding her head knowingly. "A lot of those mediums and mind readers don't always get all the information they need."

"Good God," John mumbled.

"I figured I'd find you guys here," came a woman's voice from the sidewalk.

John and Kurt looked over their shoulders.

"Hey, Cassie," Kurt said. "What brings you here?"

Violet glared at Cassie with her hands on her hips.

"I was looking for you two," said Cassie. She hopped on a stool to John's left.

"Stalking them now," Violet said snarkily.

"No. I wasn't stalking them."

Violet turned and reached for her phone.

"Do not text your mother," said John.

"I wasn't going to," Violet responded, and then laid her cell back on the back bar.

"Oh," said Cassie, "you must be Jessica Jones' daughter."

Violet nodded and sneered.

"I'm Cassie, John's neigh—"

"I know who you are."

"Would you like something to drink, Cassie?" Kurt asked.

"Yeah, Cassie," said Violet snottily, "would you like something to drink?"

"I'll just have a coffee, thanks."

Violet turned and went toward the pot of last night's coffee.

"Not that coffee," said John.

Violet sighed. "Whatever." She veered off and went into the restaurant.

"Wow, she doesn't like me any more than her mother does."

"Looks that way," said John.

"I don't know why women can never get along with each other," said Kurt.

"I don't know either," said Cassie, "but there's usually a man to blame for it."

"But it's your own damn fault," Kurt sang.

"What?" Cassie asked.

"You know," said Kurt, "like from the Jimmy Buffett song."

"Yeah, never heard it. Don't listen to dead people."

"Buffett's not dead!" Kurt exclaimed. "He's alive and better than ever."

"Anyway," John said, "why were you looking for us?"

"Remember Rosie, the girl I was telling you about, the one who dreamed about the lady who was going to die?"

"Yeah," John said, jabbing a thumb at Kurt, "this one won't let me forget about it."

"And remember I told you that she dreamed about someone else?"

"How could I forget?"

"The guy died."

"Holy crap," Kurt said, looking at his arms. "The hair on both of my arms is standing on end."

"How does Rosie know it was him?" John asked.

"She saw the guy's name in the obituary column in the paper."

"Whoa, just like last time," said Kurt.

"What could have possibly been in that obituary that made her recognize him?" John asked.

Violet returned to the bar carrying a mug of coffee. She walked behind the bar and set the mug in front of Cassie.

"There's your coffee," Violet said coldly. She looked at John. "Your breakfast will be up in a minute."

"Thanks. You want something to eat, Cassie?"

Violet rolled her eyes.

"No, thanks. I just ate."

"You're not gonna believe this, Violet," said Kurt, "but you know Rosie, the woman we were just talking about? The guy she dreamed about died."

"Are you serious?" Violet exclaimed. "She needs to go to the cops."

"She did," Cassie said. "Last night. Rosie told them about the first woman, and the guy who died yesterday."

"Let me guess," John said. "They didn't believe her."

"No, they didn't."

"I can't imagine why," said John sarcastically. "It seems like such a believable story."

"Two people have died, John," Cassie said somberly. "This isn't funny."

"No one said it was funny. And those two people would have died anyway—in an accident, from a disease, of a cold."

"Not if she could have stopped it," Kurt said.

"How could she have stopped it?" John asked.

"By letting the person know," said Violet. "Duh."

"Yeah, John, duh!" said Kurt.

"You're all insane," John told them. "All three of you."

A guy stuck his head into the bar and said, "Violet! Order's up."

"Thanks, Brian," said Violet, heading for the kitchen.

"Rosie's afraid it's going to happen again," said Cassie. "She feels responsible for their deaths. She thinks she could have prevented it."

"She couldn't have," said John. "Because she's lying."

"So, you don't believe it at all," said Kurt.

"No."

"Why?" Cassie asked.

"Because."

"Because why? If you just meet her, you'll believe her. Rosie's not a liar."

"What do you mean, if I just meet her?" John asked.

"Well, after she said the cops wouldn't listen to her, I told her about you guys."

"What about us?" John asked.

"That we're private investigators," Kurt surmised.

"Yes," said Cassie.

"But, we're not private investigators," said John.

"Well, kinda," said Kurt.

"No, not kinda. Not at all."

"Speak for yourself," said Kurt. "I investigate, and I'm private. Pretty much says I'm a private investigator."

"Pretty much just says you're going to end up eventually getting charged for practicing without a license."

"Practicing without a license," Kurt guffawed. "As if there's such a law."

"I think there is," said Cassie.

"Really? That's stupid."

Violet returned and sat their plates in front of them.

"Silverware?" Kurt asked.

Violet grabbed the napkin wrapped utensils and tossed them on the bar.

"You sure you don't want anything?" Kurt asked, as he dug into his scrambled eggs.

"I'm sure. So, when do you want to meet her?"

"I don't," said John.

"I do," Kurt said. "We gotta get to the bottom of this."

"Why would we meet her?" John asked. "What is it you think we can do for her?"

"You can help her by stopping it from happening again," Cassie said.

"Stop it how? Did her dream voices give her a name this time?"

"No, but she knows what day it's supposed to happen. It's gonna happen on Wednesday. That gives you five days to stop it."

John dropped his head back and stared at the ceiling.

"It wouldn't hurt to talk to the poor girl," said Kurt.

"Fine. We'll talk to her."

Cassie reached out and rubbed John's back. "Thank you so much," she said. "You won't regret this."

"I already do."

Chapter Three

John and Kurt arrived in Stuart at three o'clock that same afternoon. Kurt steered his van to the curb in front of a lime green bungalow on California Avenue, parking behind a black Porsche.

The two men could hear Luke Bryan singing "One Margarita" as they ascended the exterior staircase to the second-floor studio apartment where Rosie Barlow, Cassie's friend from work, lived alone.

Kurt knocked. A few seconds later the music got quieter.

"You Rosie Barlow?" Kurt asked, when the young brunette pulled open the door.

"Yeah. You John and Kurt?"

Rosie was clad only in red flannel shorts and a black sports bra. Her face and chest were sweaty, and she was breathing hard. In the harsh afternoon light, John noted a small cut and bruise above her left eye.

"I'm Kurt, and this is John."

She pulled the door all the way open and stepped back. "Come on in. Lock the door after you close it, please."

John and Kurt followed her into the apartment. They could still hear Luke Bryan, only a lot quieter. To their right was a couch, chair, end table, and television. To their left was a small round table with two chairs. Straight ahead was a six-foot sink base below a bank of wall cabinets. A small refrigerator sat to the right of the sink base, and an apartment-size stove sat to the left.

Rosie pointed toward the couch. "Please, have a seat. Would you like anything to drink?"

"No, thanks," John responded.

"Whaddaya got?" Kurt asked.

Kurt's eyes were glued to Rosie's butt as she walked to the fridge and opened it.

"I got iced tea, Diet Coke, and some White Claws," she said.

"What's a White Claw?" Kurt asked.

"It's like carbonated water with alcohol."

"I'll try that. You want one, John?"

"No, thanks."

Rosie pulled out a Black Cherry for Kurt and a Natural Lime for herself. She handed Kurt his, and set hers on the table. "Can you excuse me for one second?"

"Sure," said Kurt.

Rosie turned and walked through a door next to the stove and shut it behind her.

Kurt turned to John. "Wow!" he said. "I wonder why she's waiting tables and not up on stage dancing around that pole?"

"She's very pretty," John agreed.

"Pretty? She's about nine notches above pretty. How old ya think she is?"

"Twenty-four, maybe?"

"Think she's too young for me?"

"She's too *everything* for you, pal."

"I agree. Ya think Cassie's too young for me?"

"Ten years? I don't think so."

The bathroom door opened a few minutes later and Rosie walked out dabbing her chest with a small face towel. "I was exercising when you guys knocked," she said. She pulled one of the chairs away from the table and turned it to face Kurt and John. She picked up her White Claw and glanced dubiously at the pop-top. "Would one of you guys mind opening this for me? I don't want to break a nail. I just got these done yesterday."

John took the can, popped the top, and handed it back to her.

"Thanks." She tipped up the can and guzzled. "So, how much has Cassie told you?"

"She said you dreamed someone was going to die," said Kurt, "and then they did. Then it happened again. Cassie said you went to the police, and they thought you were a wack-job."

"One of the detectives—Helm, I think his name was—laughed at me. He asked me if aliens had come to me when I was sleeping."

"It wasn't aliens, was it?" John asked wryly.

Rosie narrowed her eyes warningly. "No, it wasn't."

Kurt asked, "Who told you these people were going to die?"

"I don't know. I never saw a face. It was just a voice."

"What exactly did the voice say?" John asked.

"I can't remember clearly, but he said—"

"It was a he?" John interrupted.

Rosie thought for a second. "Yeah, I guess it was."

"What did he say?" Kurt asked.

"I don't know. I just remember the voice, and then, when I woke up the following morning, I knew a woman was going to die."

"But you didn't know who, or when?" John probed.

"No. Not the second time either. The only thing different about the third time it happened, is that I know the woman is going to die on Wednesday."

"But no name, what she looks like, or how she's going to die?" Kurt asked.

"I'm afraid not. Do you think you can help?"

"I don't know what we can do," said John.

"We have to help this woman," Rosie said.

"There's a few hundred thousand women in the area," John stated. "Even if it is true, we have no way of knowing who it is."

"Maybe she's connected to the other two," said Rosie. She stood and went to the cupboard. She opened one of the doors and pulled out a few folded newspaper pages. "Here's the obituaries of the first two." She handed them to John. "Maybe if you can make a connection between them, you can figure out who the other person is."

"In four days," John mumbled. He handed one of the pages to Kurt.

"I circled their obits," Cassie pointed out.

Kurt read through the woman's obituary, then folded the paper.

"We'll see what we can do," he said.

"I noticed the cut over your eye," said John. "What happened?"

Rosie put her fingertips to the cut. "My boyfriend did it," she said. "He didn't mean it. It was my fault."

"It was *your* fault?" John asked.

"I just make him really mad sometimes."

"This happen before?" Kurt asked.

"Yes. I mean, no … not like this. He didn't hit me. He pushed me and I tripped. I hit my head on the edge of the table. I'm so clumsy."

"When did it happen?" John asked.

"A couple weeks ago. It's almost healed up."

"Did you start having these dreams after you hit your head?" John asked.

"What do you mean?"

"I mean, did you start hearing voices after you smacked your head on the table?"

"It wasn't that bad. And it's almost healed up now."

"Not from where I'm standing. It must have been pretty bad."

Rosie drew herself up. "Look," she bristled, "I didn't ask you here to judge my boyfriend and my relationship. If you don't want to do this, just say so."

"I'm not judging anyone. If you want to date some douche who slaps you around, that's fine with me." John stood. "I'll be in the van," he said, and walked out the door.

"He's kind of a jerk," said Rosie.

"Not usually," said Kurt. "I don't know what his problem is today."

"So, are you going to help this woman … whoever she is?"

"We'll do what we can, Rosie," Kurt assured her. "I'll call if I have any more questions."

"Thank you." Rosie stood when Kurt did. She put her arms around him and squeezed. She rose on her tiptoes and kissed the lanky guy on his reddening cheek. "Thank you so much."

Kurt couldn't quit grinning. *Maybe I do have a shot with her,* he thought.

The two separated, and Rosie looked into Kurt's eyes. "My dad passed away when I was a kid," she said.

"I'm sorry to hear that," Kurt replied, swallowing the frog in his throat.

"You remind me so much of him."

"I do?"

"Yeah. He had long, curly hair like yours. He'd even be about your same age, if he were still alive. Yeah, it's just like my dad is here in the room with me. Weird."

"Yeah, weird," said Kurt, abruptly taking his leave.

John was leaning up against the van's passenger side door when Kurt, scowling, descended the stairs two at a time. Without a word, he leapt inside and started it. John barely had time to climb into the passenger seat before Kurt sped off.

"What's the matter with you?" John finally asked his friend. "You haven't said a word since we left Rosie's."

"Nothing's the matter."

"Something's the matter."

"I don't want to talk about it."

"So, there is something wrong."

"Stop."

"What is it?"

"Drop it." Kurt hung a right off US1, onto Baker Road.

"Did Rosie say something?"

"She said I reminded her of her father! She said I'm the same age he would be if he hadn't passed away. She even said he had long, curly hair like mine, and that she felt like he was standing in the room with her."

"That must have stung."

"No shit. I don't picture myself being that old."

"You're not that old, just a lot older than her."

"That makes me feel better." Kurt reached down and turned on the radio. He fiddled with the dial until he found a song he liked—*Paint it Black*, by the Rolling Stones. He hung his arm out the window and tapped his thumb on the door to the beat.

John spent the drive reading through the two obituaries Rosie had given them. "Says here Vicky Cady was forty-nine when she died," he said. "She's survived by her two children. Daughter's name is Lauren Hammett. Her husband's name is Conner. Son's name is Doug Cady. Doesn't look like the son's married. Vicky has two grandchildren—doesn't give their names."

"Vicky married?" Kurt asked.

"I just said her husband's name was Conner. Pay attention."

"I thought you meant her daughter's husband was Conner. Does it say what she did for a living?"

"No, but it does say she was enjoying her retirement, and some of her favorite activities were hiking, running, kayaking, and paddle boarding."

"How'd she die?"

"Just says she died unexpectedly."

"Ya know what we forgot to ask Rosie?"

"What's that?"

"What was it about Vicky's obituary that made her realize it was the person she had dreamed about?"

"Yeah, I wondered about that, because there's nothing unusual in this obit that would make Vicky stand out."

John folded the paper and shuffled it underneath Friday's obituary, and began reading that one.

Kurt took a left at Mulligan's and sped up Indian River Drive. By the time John glanced up from the newspaper, Kurt had steered the hippie van onto Causeway Boulevard and was heading toward Hutchinson Island.

"Where're we going?" John asked.

"Breakwater Bar and Grill," Kurt replied.

"Why?"

"To speak with our new friend Cole Ballinger."

"About what?"

"I want to know how Vicky Cady died. Who better to ask than a retired cop. Besides, he owes us one."

"How do you figure he owes us one?"

"Because we helped him with the Kimberly Levesque case."

"Kurt, we didn't really help him. He would have done just fine without us."

"What are you talking about? He probably never would have gotten in to see Alfredo Fettuccine, if Fettuccine wasn't such a big fan of yours."

"It's Alfredino Fallaci, not Alfredo Fettuccine."

"Close enough. By the way, I can't believe you didn't take that twenty-grand Ballinger tried to give you."

"It was stolen money."

"Stolen from a bad cop."

"Doesn't matter. Stolen is stolen. Besides, I figured Kimberly Levesque's parents could use the money."

"You're such a Boy Scout."

"I think you know I was only a Boy Scout for less than a week."

"Yes, I seem to recall you got into a little bit of trouble."

"*I* got into trouble? You got *me* into trouble."

Kurt shrugged. "Sorry. Who would have ever thought that carrying a coffee can around door to door collecting for charity was illegal."

"It is when you're dressed in your Boy Scout uniform and that charity is bogus."

"Yeah," Kurt chuckled. "You'd think the name Scouts for Scabies would have raised some red flags. Suckers!"

"And to top it off, we spent all the money on two new skateboards."

"Those were some bitchin' boards. Too bad we had to give them back. Sometimes, if I sit just right, I can still feel the sting where my dad hit me with that belt."

"I know what you mean."

"Yeah, like either one of your parents ever hit you."

"The fear of getting smacked was worse."

"Trust me, it wasn't."

"And yet you never learned. Now that I think of it, every time I got into trouble as a kid it was because we were doing something stupid that you thought up."

"Wait a minute. It was your idea to cut the roof off your old Dodge Dart because you wanted a convertible."

"Yeah, that was my idea." John laughed. "No roof and going down a one-way street the wrong way. The look on that cop's face. I thought he was going to shoot me. Grabbed me by the front of the shirt and yanked me right out of the car."

"What was that cop's name?"

"Officer Bolan," John recalled. "I wonder what ever happened to that guy?"

"I wonder if he ever watched *Law of the Land* and told his wife, 'I dragged that little bastard out of his car one night for going the wrong way down a one-way street.'"

John chuckled. "I wonder."

Chapter Four

Twenty-five minutes later Kurt drove his van down Seaway Drive and around Jetty Park. He pulled into a parking spot right beside Cole Ballinger's Ford pickup.

"He's here," John said. "This is his truck right next to us."

"Of course he's here," said Kurt. "He's got a business to run. Where else would he be?"

With his hand on the door handle, John looked over at his friend. "You also have a business to run, and you're never there."

"Bah," Kurt said, waving him off. "That place practically runs itself."

"You mean Sara runs the place. She seems to be there every day from the time it opens until it closes."

"She's a great employee. Puts in a lot of hours. Would you believe she makes more than me most weeks? And I own the place."

"I wouldn't doubt it."

The two men hopped out of the van and walked across Jetty Park to the front door of the Breakwater Bar and Grill. Kurt had the obituaries tucked into his armpit.

"Listen," John said, as they walked along. "Don't mention that twenty grand to anyone, not even Cole."

"Why, what's the problem?"

"His cook—that Leon guy. He said if I told anyone about the money, they'd find me in a dumpster."

"Are ya shittin' me?"

"No, and I believe him, so mum's the word."

"Did he say you would be dead when they found you in the dumpster?"

"I didn't ask, but I assumed so."

"Huh. That's scary."

"Yeah, and *he's* scary."

John pulled the door open, and Kurt walked in first.

Cole was behind the bar, leaning against the back bar, with his foot up on the bar sink. He did a double take when he saw John and Kurt walk in.

"Well, look what the cat dragged in," said Cole. "Haven't seen you guys in a few weeks. How're the ribs, Kurt?"

"Still a little tender," Kurt replied.

John pulled out a stool three to the right of an old man who was pulling dollar bills out of a clear sandwich bag. John nodded to the old guy. The old guy nodded back.

"What can I get you guys?" Cole asked.

"LandShark," Kurt replied.

"Yeah, me too, please," said John.

Cole turned and grabbed the bottles out of the cooler and twisted off the tops. "There ya go," he said, setting the beers in front of them. "Can I get you a couple menus?"

"Yeah, I'm starving," said John.

Cole grabbed two menus off the back bar and tossed them on the bar. "So, what brings you boys in?" he asked. "I mean, besides the superb food and drink. Rated best in Fort Pierce by Zagat."

"Really?" said John.

Cole snorted. "What do you think?"

Kurt tossed the obituaries on the bar and sat down to John's right. "Two dead people," he said.

"I knew it was something crazy," said Cole. He glanced down at the newspapers. "Obituaries?"

"Yep," Kurt said.

Cole unfolded the newspapers and placed them side by side in front of him. What he was supposed to see was obvious, because the names had been circled with a red Sharpie. He skimmed Vicky Cady's write-up for a second, and then his eyes wondered over to Elliott Guston's obituary.

"What about them?" Cole asked.

"I'll let *him* tell you," said John.

"Our client—"

"Our client," John mocked. "Now, tell Cole how much *our client* is paying us." He made a goose egg with his thumb and finger.

"That's beside the point," Kurt said. "Our client dreamed that these two people were going to die, and then they did."

Cole's face remained expressionless. "And?"

"That's not enough?"

"No. I can do that too." Cole put his index and middle finger to his temple and concentrated as hard as he could. After seven or eight seconds he pointed at Kurt and said, "You're going to die." His finger swung around to John. "You're also going to die." He then pointed his finger at the old guy at the end of the bar. "And, Melvin, you're going to die … probably a lot sooner than these two, because you're so friggin old."

"Shove that finger up your ass, Ballinger," Melvin Mulhern said. "I'll probably outlive all of ya."

"See how easy that was?" Cole asked. "I just predicted all of your deaths. Now we just sit back and wait."

John chuckled.

Kurt nodded his head toward John. "You sound just like this guy."

"How did you expect me to sound?" Cole asked.

"You used to be a cop. I thought you'd find it interesting."

"What am I missing here?"

"The woman dreamt about their deaths a few days before they died," John explained. "You're not missing anything."

"Why didn't she warn them?" Cole asked.

"That's what everybody asks," John said.

"Because she didn't know their names," Kurt chimed in. "She recognized them from their obituaries."

"You mean she recognized them by their photographs?"

"No, by what was written about them."

Cole studied Vicky Cady's obituary. "What in this write-up made your allegedly clairvoyant client think it was the person she dreamed about?"

"We forgot to ask her that," Kurt said.

Cole slid the papers back across the bar to Kurt. "Maybe you'd better ask her that question."

"Is there any way you could find out how this lady died?" Kurt asked. "All it says is that she died unexpectedly. Elliott Guston's obit just says that he died with his family at his side."

"His *loving* family," Cole corrected. "Everyone's *loving* family is always at their bedside. You never hear about anyone's *hateful* family. As a matter of fact, I see he also died peacefully. They never say anyone dies kicking and screaming as they were dragged by the Grim Reaper through the gates of hell."

"That *would* make for juicier reading," John agreed.

"I searched both names online," said Kurt. "Only their obituaries come up."

Cole sighed. "I'll make a couple calls."

"Thanks."

"Did your client talk to the cops about this?"

"Yes. They laughed at her."

"I can't imagine why," Cole deadpanned. "Sounds legit to me. I'm surprised they didn't put this client of yours on the payroll. Just think of the lives she could save if only she'd dream up the names."

"He hasn't told you the best part," John said.

"There's a best part?" Cole inquired. "I can't wait. I'm positively giddy."

"She had another dream. This time it's a woman, and the woman is going to die on Wednesday."

"Which Wednesday?"

"This coming Wednesday."

"How does she know it's this coming Wednesday?"

"Uh … we forgot to ask her that too," Kurt admitted.

"No wonder you're getting paid bupkis." Cole grabbed a notepad behind him and jotted down both names. "Like I said, I'll make a couple calls for you."

"I just figured if we could find some connection between these two," Kurt explained, "maybe we could save the next person."

"That's how I'd go about it," said Cole.

"Ya mean, if this was your case?" Kurt asked.

"Oh, no, I wouldn't take a case this stupid. I meant, that's how I'd go about it if I was you."

"Oh."

"But what even makes you think there's a connection between these two?" Cole asked.

"The client put it in his head," said John.

"I was thinkin' it before she said it," Kurt responded.

"Sure you were," John said. "All you were thinkin' was about her butt."

"Well, yeah, that was one of the things I was thinkin' about."

Cole snorted. "Did ya decide what you want to eat?"

"I'll have a cheeseburger and fries," said John.

"Me too," said Kurt.

"Norma!" Cole hollered into the dining room, startling the sixty-something brunette waiting on a two-top.

"What?" she asked, spinning around. She had a hook nose that John observed privately, looked capable of opening a tuna can.

"Can you run into the kitchen and tell Leon to make me two cheeseburgers with fries?"

Norma stared emotionlessly at Cole for a few seconds. Finally, she just turned back around to her table, completely ignoring her boss.

Cole gazed at the back of Norma's head. "Ya know what? Maybe I'll just run this order in myself." He walked around the bar and elbowed past the swinging door into the kitchen.

A beautiful blonde woman walked through the entrance door, seemingly bringing the Florida sunshine with her. She lingered for a moment in the foyer, putting her keys in her purse, bathed in an angelic golden glow. Kurt jabbed John in the ribs to get him to take a gander.

"You're too old for her as well," John stated.

"She's gotta be, like, twenty-five," Kurt argued.

"Yeah, I know. We need to find you a woman who's at least thirty-five."

The blonde vision stepped behind the bar. She looked at everyone's drinks.

"You guys ready for another?" she asked, tying her apron around her waist.

"We're good for now," John answered. "Thank you."

She looked to the end of the bar. "Are ya ready, Mr. Mulhern?" she asked.

He lifted his glass and swirled its contents. The ice had completely melted. "Not quite, princess," said the old prune.

Cole returned to the bar a few moments later. He walked around behind the young woman, and leaned against the back bar.

"I like this bartender way better than you, Cole," said Kurt. "She's a lot prettier."

"Well, Allison's my daughter," Cole replied. "So, her good looks come from me."

"I don't see the resemblance at all."

Allison snickered. "Everyone says I look like my mom," she said.

"She must be a beautiful woman."

"On the outside," Cole grumbled.

"Dad," Allison scolded.

"Sorry."

"I take it the two of you aren't together anymore," said John.

"Nope," Cole said. "We've been divorced for quite some time."

"Girlfriend?" Kurt asked.

"Yes."

"You have a boyfriend, Allison?"

"God, you're nosy," John said.

"Yes, I have a boyfriend," Allison responded.

"He's a cop," said Cole. He paused for a beat, added: "With a gun and an itchy trigger finger."

"I was just curious."

"Well, don't be," Cole said. "What are you, thirty-five?"

"Forty-two, but thanks."

Allison reached out and picked up one of the newspapers. She saw that one of the obituaries was circled.

"This a friend of yours, Daddy?" she asked.

"No," Kurt replied. "We're investigating that woman's death."

"Investigating," Cole mumbled.

"You're detectives?" asked Allison.

"No," said her father, "they're not. They're just regular guys who like sticking their nose in other people's business."

Allison looked up from the newspaper and stared at John for a few seconds. "You look familiar," she said.

"I was in here a couple times a few weeks ago," John told her.

"No, other than that."

"Ya mean, you really don't know who this is?" Kurt asked.

Allison shook her head.

"Have you ever heard of a television show called *Law of the Land*?"

"Yeah, my dad watched it every—hey, you're Mason Land!"

John nodded his head.

"Oh my God!" said Allison. "Dad, you loved that show."

"I wouldn't say, loved," Cole responded. "It was okay."

"Okay? You never missed an episode. I remember you calling home to make sure mom recorded it."

"That's enough," Cole said. "He doesn't want to hear about all that."

"No, no," John insisted, "you go ahead, Allison. I do like hearing this. Because when I first met your father, he referred to my TV show as, and I quote, 'A stupid cop show. God, I hated that show. So unrealistic, and that guy couldn't act his way out of a wet paper bag.' Isn't that what you said, Cole?"

Cole's face reddened a shade. "I may have said something along those lines, but—"

"But," said Kurt, interrupting, "you're actually a fan."

"I wouldn't say, a fan."

"Dad, who are you trying to kid?" said Allison. "You were a big fan of Mr. Burton's. Remember when you bought those ridiculously overpriced Oliver Peoples sunglasses just like Mason La—"

Cole quickly cut her off. "Don't you have something you should be doing right now, Allison?" he asked. "Are the bathrooms mopped?"

"I don't mop the bathrooms when I work the afternoon shift."

"Today you do," said Cole, pointing toward the hallway that led to his office and the restrooms.

Sighing, Allison walked around the bar. "It was nice to meet you Mr. Burton," she said.

"Nice to meet you, Allison. Call me John."

Allison walked to the kitchen and disappeared through the swinging door.

"Big fan, huh?" said Kurt.

"I have a gun on my hip right now," Cole warned.

Chapter Five

It was Saturday afternoon, about two o'clock, when John's cell phone rang. He picked up the phone and turned it so Kurt could see the screen. The friends were lounging poolside, as usual.

"It's Cole," John said.

"I see that," Kurt replied. "Answer it."

"Hello?"

"Hey, John, it's Cole Ballinger. I asked about those two people. Vicky Cady took a tumble down her stairs, broke her neck, was dead at the scene. It was an accident, nothing suspicious. Elliott Guston died after a two-year battle with cancer."

"Any connection between the two of them?" John asked.

"Nothing obvious, but that's for you guys to figure out."

"How am I supposed to go about that? We can't just show up at the deceased's house and start asking questions."

"Not without a believable reason."

"So, you're saying we should make something up?"

"I'm not saying anything."

"If you were saying something, what would you say?"

"I don't know. You're from the insurance company, or something. Maybe an old friend who's come to pay your condolences."

"Or we could just drop it."

"You could do that."

"Would you?"

"Probably."

"You have addresses on both of them?"

"Yeah. Cady lives at—"

"Wait, I don't have a pen or paper. Can you text me the addresses?"

"Of course. It's not like I have anything better to do. Anything else?"

"If you want a cold beer you can stop over to my place. Kurt and I are just sitting by the pool."

"Of course you are. I'll be right over."

John stared at his cell phone for a minute or so, waiting for the text message from Cole; it never came. He put the phone back on the table where he got it.

"Another beer?" John asked.

"Shore," Kurt replied. He was lying down on a lounge chair with a beach towel over his face.

John sat up and opened the ice chest that was sitting at the end of his lounge. He reached inside and pulled out two LandSharks. "Why have you got that towel over your face?" he asked.

"The sun ages you, pal. I gotta keep my youthful appearance."

"One person guesses your age a few years younger than it actually is, and now you have a youthful appearance?"

"Almost ten years younger."

Kurt had his arm extended and his hand open, eagerly awaiting John handing him his beer. When he finally felt the wet, cold bottle hit his palm, he closed his hand.

"Thanks," said Kurt. He pulled the towel off his face, sat up a little, and took a swig. "It doesn't get any better than this."

"You say that every day."

"And I mean it every day. What did Cole have to say?"

"Vicky Cady fell down her stairs at home—broke her neck. Elliott Guston died after a two-year illness."

"Any connection between the two?"

"He said that's for us to find out."

"Huh."

"He's on his way over."

"Was Vicky Cady alone in her house when she fell down the stairs?"

"I don't know. Why?"

"Maybe she was pushed."

"Why would you say that? Nothing about Rosie's dream said murder, just that she was going to die."

"That wouldn't make sense."

"Why wouldn't it?"

"Because, why would someone dream about someone's death if it wasn't going to be murder. It's always murder in predictions like that."

"Predictions like what? You think this is something that happens all the time?"

"Probably more than we know."

"You're probably more wacky than we know."

"Probably."

"Elliott Guston obviously wasn't murdered. He died of cancer."

"Maybe someone held a pillow over his face and suffocated him."

"With his loving family at his side?"

"Maybe it was his loving family who killed him. Maybe he had a fortune and the loving family all got together and decided to kill him to get the money. So they held a pillow over his face."

"You've got some imagination. Maybe someone should hold a pillow over your face."

"Probably. But, this reminds me of a joke."

"I'm sure it does."

"This guy was on trial for killing his wife, even though no body had been found. His lawyer tells the jury, 'You can't convict my client. There's not enough evidence—there's no body. She's still alive. As a matter of fact, my client's wife is going to walk through that door any second.' He turns and points at the door. Everyone on the jury turns their head and stares at the door. They waited, and waited, but the door never opened. Finally the judge says, 'Where is she?' 'I have no idea,' says the lawyer, 'but the fact that you were all staring at the door proves there is reasonable doubt.' The jury leaves, and returns fifteen minutes later with a guilty verdict. The guy's lawyer says, 'How can you convict my client on such flimsy evidence?" The head juror replies, 'Next time you try that trick, make sure to tell your *client* to turn around and look at the door.'"

"Brilliant," said John. He tipped up his beer bottle.

Kurt was still laughing at his own joke and holding his ribs when he stood up. He took one quick glance toward Cassie's house. She was nowhere in sight. He walked to the edge of the pool.

"Don't dive," John said.

"Why?"

"You hurt yourself last time."

"Now I know the right way to do it."

"Is the right way *not* diving?"

"No."

"Then it's the wrong way."

Pfft! Kurt dove in. When he resurfaced there was the obvious look of a moron in pain.

"What's the matter?" John asked.

"Nothing," Kurt gasped.

"Doesn't sound like nothing."

"I'm fine." Kurt moved to the side of the pool and tried to lift himself out. "Ahhh!" He cried out. "Son of a bitch."

"Maybe you should try using the steps."

"Maybe you should try using the steps," Kurt parroted, on his way to the steps. He walked back to his lounge chair and sat down. "There, it's all good."

"Yeah, it looked all good. Your face is pale. Paler than usual, that is, Casper."

A few minutes later Cole Ballinger walked around the corner of the house. He was wearing cargo shorts and a T-shirt.

"Did ya bring your trunks?" Kurt asked.

Cole threw up his index finger and spun around. "They're in the truck," he said. He walked back to the truck, and returned with his swim trunks in his hand.

No sooner had Cole sat down in one of the unoccupied lounge chairs than, Cassie's back door slammed shut. The three men turned their heads to see the stunning woman walking toward them. She was carrying a newspaper in her hand.

"Who's that?" Cole asked.

"My neighbor," John replied.

"A stripper," Kurt added.

"You don't have to tell everyone she's a stripper," John said. "And I think she prefers the term exotic dancer."

"Why?" Kurt asked. "Stripping is an honorable profession."

Cole's eyes were glued to the Venus strutting across the yards. "Especially when God built you like that," he said in an awed whisper. "Glory hallelujah!"

Cassie tossed the newspaper on the table, on top of John's cell phone. "There it is," she said. "Rosie made a little mistake." She looked at Cole. "Hey."

Cole tucked his eyes back in their sockets and smiled. "Hey,"

"A mistake?" John asked. "What are you talking about?"

"The guy who died," Cassie explained. "Wrong guy. It was someone else."

"What do you mean, someone else?" Kurt asked.

"That Guston guy. Rosie thought he was the guy she dreamed about, but she was wrong. This is the guy." Cassie pointed at the newspaper. "She's positive this time."

John picked it up and unfolded it. Mark Steuben's obituary was circled in red ink.

He tossed the paper back on the table. "I don't care," he said. "I'm out. This is stupid."

"What makes her think that's the guy?" Cole asked.

Cassie sniffed. "Who the hell are you, by the way?"

"Cole Ballinger."

"He's a friend of ours," said Kurt.

"You a cop?" Cassie asked. "You look like a cop."

"You look like a stripper," Cole said. "You a stripper?"

Cassie's mouth opened, and then closed.

"He's a detective," John said. "Pretty good, huh?"

"Are you being a dick?" Cassie asked.

"Usually," Cole responded. "You don't like dicks?"

Cassie grinned. "You *are* a dick."

"I try my hardest."

"I bet you don't have to try at all."

Cole laughed. "I like her," he told John.

Cassie looked at Kurt. "Did you tell him I was an exotic dancer?"

"No," said Kurt.

"Did you tell him I was a stripper?"

"Yes."

"What makes Rosie think this is the guy?" John asked.

"And what makes her so sure she had it wrong the first time?" Cole asked.

Cole held out his hand for the newspaper, and John picked it up and handed it to him.

"Rosie said she took one look at Steuben's name," Cassie said, "and remembered she had heard it in her dream."

"But she didn't remember the name before she saw it?" Kurt asked.

"No."

"I wonder if that's how she knew the first victim was Vicky Cady."

"Stop calling them victims," John insisted. "They're just people who died."

"I asked her that same question, string bean. She said she doesn't remember hearing the name Vicky Cady in her dream, but anything is possible."

"Says here the guy was a victim of a hit-and-run," Cole said.

"Ha!" said Kurt. "See, the guy was a victim. That makes two suspicious deaths."

"Suspicious?" said John. "What's suspicious about tripping and falling down your stairs? I'm sure people do it all the time."

"Twelve thousand folks per year," said Kurt.

"How the hell did you know that, string bean?" Cassie asked.

Kurt held up his cell phone. "Just Googled it."

"See, twelve thousand people," John said. "And how many of those are murder?"

"How would they know? It's the perfect crime," Kurt said.

"I have to say," Cole said, "I was in law enforcement for a lot of years, and that's the first time I ever heard 'falling down the stairs' described as *the perfect crime.*"

"Like they say, first time for everything," Kurt pointed out.

"Yeah, but probably not this," Cole responded.

"You think you can get us a look at the police report?" Kurt asked.

"No," Cole replied.

"Can you get us this guy's address?"

"Google it. You got one of those beers for me?"

"Oh, yeah, sorry," John said. He flipped open the cooler and pulled out a beer. "Here ya go. You want one, Cassie?"

"No, thanks, John. I gotta get to work."

"This early?"

"The girl who goes in at four called in sick, so I have to cover."

"So, you'll be dancing for nine hours?" Kurt asked.

"I guess so."

Picturing Cassie on stage, Kurt's eyes glazed over and his lips twitched spasmodically like a cat ogling a bird.

Cassie snapped her fingers. "Hey, beanpole, come back to earth!"

"Oh, sorry," Kurt said. "My mind was wandering. Wait—beanpole? I thought it was string bean."

"I can't make up my mind which one I like better."

John and Cole laughed.

"Well, I better get changed and get to work," Cassie said.

"Have a nice time," said Kurt.

"Oh, yeah," Cassie responded, "I'll have a spectacular time. A bar full of old guys saying rude shit to me and trying to cop a feel while stuffing ones in my G-string. What more could a girl ask for?"

"Hey," Cole said, "that kinda hurts. We're old guys."

"Speak for yourself," said Kurt. "I look ten years younger than I am."

"Trust me," said Cassie, "the way those guys act, and the way you guys act, are two totally different things. Ya know what, on second thought, I think I will have that beer."

John twisted the top off a beer and handed it to Cassie. She upended the bottle and guzzled down half of it.

"I don't think any of those douchebags will notice if I'm drunk," she said.

"You're probably right," said Kurt. He looked her up and down. "They won't notice that at all."

"Okay, beanpole, I take it back. Maybe you are as creepy as some of those old guys."

"You may think that's an insult, but creepy is actually a step up for me."

Chapter Six

John pulled his Jeep Wrangler to the curb in front of a gray, ranch-style home on Roberta Street, in Jensen Beach. All six windows in the front of the house were covered by white hurricane shutters. The name on the mailbox said STEUBEN. Mark Steuben had what was arguably the most well-manicured lawn on Roberta Street.

"I really don't think we should be bothering this poor woman on the weekend like this," said John.

"Why not?" Kurt asked. "It's not like she has plans for the weekend. Her husband just died."

Shaking his head, John looked over at his pal. Kurt was fumbling with his wallet.

"What are you doing?" John asked.

"I bought this new wallet yesterday," Kurt answered. He flipped open the wallet a few times. "Looks more like a wallet a detective would have."

"Brilliant."

Kurt flipped the wallet open again. "See, my ID is right there, and the badge would go above it."

"Only, you don't have a badge."

"No, but I was thinking if I open and close it fast enough, they won't notice."

John leaned in to have a closer look at the ID. "Detective Dirk Stone," he read. "I think you may have lost your damn mind."

"I don't want to use my real name." Kurt swung open the passenger side door. "Let's rock and roll."

The two men got out of the Jeep and strolled up the gravel driveway to the front door. Kurt knocked.

A woman in her early fifties opened the door. "Yes?"

"Mrs. Steuben?" Kurt said.

"Yes."

Kurt quickly flashed his ID and returned the wallet to his back pocket. "I'm Detective Dirk Stone, and this is my partner, Detective Brock Storm. We're working with the Martin County Sheriff's Department. Would it be okay if we came in and asked you a few questions?"

The woman looked Kurt up and down. "Detectives?"

"Yes."

"Dressed like that?"

Kurt looked down at his board shorts and flop-flops. "We're under cover, ma'am."

"Oh, I see. Is this about Mark?"

"Yes."

"Please, come in."

When the woman turned around, Kurt looked back over his shoulder at John. "We're in," he whispered.

"Please, have a seat," said Mrs. Steuben, pointing at two chairs in the living room, across from the sofa. "Can I get you gentlemen something to drink? Coffee, perhaps, or sweet tea?"

"No, thank you," John answered as he sat down in one of the floral-patterned chairs.

"I'll take a sweet tea," said Kurt. He plopped down in the chair to John's left.

"I'll be right back with that," Mrs. Steuben said, and headed down the hallway.

"Hey," Kurt whispered. He pulled a small notebook and pen out of his side pocket.

"What?" said John.

"We don't know what the car looks like that hit him."

"So?"

"How do I tell her it's been spotted somewhere?"

"That's the plan?"

"Yeah, they always do that on cop shows. I figured you'd know that, what with you starring in a cop show of your own."

"Just ask her what the car looked like."

"Then I'll sound like I don't know what I'm talking about."

"Before you question her, warn her that you'll probably ask a few questions that she's already been asked."

"Great idea."

"I had a cop show of my own."

"What do you think of my new notepad? Pretty sweet, huh?"

"Pretty sweet."

"Here you are," Mrs. Steuben said, setting Kurt's sweet tea on the end table between the two chairs.

"Thanks," said Kurt. He grabbed the glass, took a sip, and smiled ingratiatingly. "Sweet as mama's kisses. Just the way I like it." John suppressed a groan.

Mrs. Steuben sat across from them on the sofa. "Now, what can I do for you gentlemen?" she asked.

"Let me start by saying, I'm very sorry for your loss, Mrs. Steuben," said Kurt.

"Thank you, but please, call me Margie."

"Very well, Margie. I apologize in advance for the line of questioning I'm obliged to undertake. A few questions are ones I'm sure you've already been asked, while others may be little painful."

Margie nodded. "It's okay. I understand."

"First of all, please describe the vehicle that struck your husband."

"It was a dark car—black or gray. It was a four door. The other police officers showed me photographs of several types of cars. I think it was a Chevy Impala."

Kurt scribbled it down in his notebook. "Now, walk us through exactly what happened that morning."

"Well, we got up at the usual time and—"

"This was last Tuesday?" John interjected.

"Yes."

"Go ahead," Kurt prompted.

"We got up, had our coffee, and around seven, we went for a run. Mark had never been a runner until I encouraged him, for his health. He started the week after he retired. When he first started, he couldn't keep up with me at all. He was so discouraged at first. He kept at it and after a few months, he was running right alongside me. I never let on that I was running slower than usual so he could keep up."

"How long ago did Mark retire?" Kurt asked.

"April, and I retired in June—exactly two months to the day after he retired."

"Where did Mark work?"

"He was head of maintenance at Palm Garden."

"Palm Garden?"

"It's an assisted living facility in Port Saint Lucie."

Kurt nodded as he jotted it down in his notebook. "And where did you retire from?"

"Thirty years with Bank of America. Most recently at the branch on the corner of US-1 and Jensen Beach Boulevard."

"So, you went for a run," John said. "Then what happened?"

"We were running along Media Avenue—that's right down here at the end of our street—and just as we were getting to Marian Street, this car comes barreling around the corner. He didn't even slow down for the stop sign. He swerved to miss me, and hit Mark."

"Was Mark conscious at all after the accident?" John asked.

"He was in and out."

"Was he able to speak to you?" Kurt asked.

"No. He just lay there on his back staring into my eyes. I kept telling him I loved him, and that the ambulance would be there any second. He closed his eyes again just before the ambulance got there. I think he passed while I was holding his hand."

Kurt, scribbling, asked without looking up, "Who called 911?"

"The woman who saw it happen. She lives right on the corner of Marian and Media. There's a blacktop driveway cut into her front yard. That's where Mark landed. She was working out in her front yard and saw the whole thing happen. Can't remember her name."

"We'll look for her name in the police report," said Kurt.

"Did you and Mark run the same route every day?" John asked.

"Yes," said Margie, thinking about it. "We would usually run to the end of the street, turn up Media Avenue, and then sometimes we'd switch it up a little, but not often."

"Did you run on the same days, around the same time?"

"Pretty much."

Kurt continued to write in his notebook as John asked questions.

"In your opinion, was there anything about the accident that seemed deliberate?"

"You mean, did he hit Mark on purpose?"

John nodded.

"No, it seemed like an accident. Is there some reason you believe it *was* on purpose?"

"No, it's just that when it's a hit and run like this, we try to cover all the bases."

"I see."

"Had Mark been threatened by anyone recently?" John asked.

"Threatened? Of course not. Who would threaten him?"

"It could be anything," John explained. "An argument with someone in a grocery store, retaliation for a road rage incident. The most insignificant event to you or Mark could have triggered someone to seek retaliation. If you can think of anything along those lines that might have happened over the past few weeks, it could be helpful."

Margie's brow furrowed in thought. "Nothing comes immediately to mind."

Kurt reached for his new wallet. He opened one of the slots and pulled out a business card. "If you do think of anything else, don't hesitate to give us a call," he said, handing Margie the card. "Like John said, it could be the smallest thing."

John's eyes widened.

"Who's John?" Margie asked.

"I mean, Detective Storm," said Kurt, with a fake chuckle. "John's his nickname."

"Oh, I see."

Kurt stood, prompting John and Margie to follow suit. "Thank you very much for your time," Kurt said. "and once again, so sorry for your loss." John concurred with a plastered-on smile.

Margie walked the phony detectives to the door, and they walked back down the gravel driveway to John's Jeep.

"Like John said," John grumbled as he started the Wrangler.

"Yeah," said Kurt, "that was a close one."

"Now she knows my real name."

"Relax. Just your first name. We're lucky she didn't recognize you from the tube."

John steered away from the curb.

"Where'd you get the business cards?" John asked.

"Office Depot."

"Business cards, fake ID, impersonating a police officer. You're going to prison."

"For helping people, John? They don't just stick folks in prison for helping others. If anything, we deserve another award."

John hung a left onto Media Avenue.

"Where did you get the fake ID?" John asked.

"I printed that off myself at the store. Pretty convincing, huh?"

"Yeah, I'm convinced you're crazy."

"I wonder where I can get a badge?"

John slowed the Jeep as they neared Marian Street. "This must be where the woman who called 911 lives," he said.

"Yeah," said Kurt, "there's the driveway cut-out where Steuben landed."

John pulled over and shut off the engine. "Might as well see what she has to say."

The two men walked up the sidewalk to the front door. There were no cars in the driveway. John knocked. He waited about a minute and knocked again.

"Doesn't look like anyone's home," said Kurt.

John knocked once more. "Yeah, I think you're right."

The two men returned to the Jeep and sped off.

"What's for supper?" Kurt asked.

"I'm supposed to meet Jessica at Mulligan's around six," John replied.

Kurt looked at his wristwatch. "Sounds good to me," he said. "I assume you were inviting me along."

"Of course," John joked. "What would a meal be like without you?"

"I hope you never have to find out, my friend. By the way, can you stop at Family Dollar on the way?"

"Sure. What do you need?"

"I was gonna see if they had any police badges."

"I'm sure they do. That's where all the cops buy their badges."

Kurt laughed. "I bet they do. I meant maybe a kid's police badge. That would be good enough to fool most people."

"Speaking of fake, do you think it's a good idea to have your phone number on a business card?"

Kurt grinned as he fished inside the side pocked of his board shorts. He yanked out a flip phone. "Burner phone," he said. "Can't be traced back to me."

"It can," John informed him, "if you used a debit or credit card to buy it at a place with security cameras."

"Why would anyone go through all that trouble to find me?"

"I know, because all you're doing is helping people."

"Correctamundo, my friend."

Chapter Seven

John and Kurt sat at the bar at Mulligan's. John had a pint of Sunrise City IPA in front of him. Kurt was halfway through a bottle of Bud Light.

"How many times are you going to do that?" John asked his friend.

Kurt flipped his wallet open to reveal his chrome-like, plastic badge. "As many times as it takes me to make it look legit." He flashed the badge one more time to Violet. "Detective Dirk Stone," he said, in his best Clint Eastwood voice.

"Don't say it like that," said Violet. "It sounds creepy."

"Don't I sound like Clint Eastwood?" Kurt asked.

"It all depends," Violet answered. "Is Clint Eastwood a creepy old man?"

"No! He's awesome."

"Then no, you don't sound like him."

John burst out laughing.

Kurt handed the wallet to John. "Here, you do it."

"I'm not doing it," John protested.

"Just say it like you said it on your show."

John reluctantly snatched the wallet and badge away from his friend. He mimicked pulling the badge from his vest pocket. "Detective Mason Land," he said, affecting a deep, virile voice and flashing the badge. "LAPD."

Kurt's jaw dropped. "That. Was. Awesome!"

John glanced over at Violet. She was grinning big. "That was pretty cool, John," she assured him. "Just like watching your show."

"Thanks."

"Ya know, John," Kurt said, "I just thought of something."

"Yeah, what's that?"

"Why have they never done a *Law of the Land* movie? Like a reunion, with the original cast?"

"It was canceled for low ratings, Kurt. Who would watch it?"

"Everyone who loved it back then. I would watch it."

"Me and my mom would watch," said Violet.

"Thanks, guys, but the show ended almost ten years ago. No one would watch."

"Sure they would, pal. *And,* I have another idea."

"Can't wait to hear it."

"Ya know the screenplay we've been working on?"

"You mean the one *I've* been working on?"

"Whatever. What if the plot revolved around Mason Land, on vacation in Jensen Beach? He runs into an old friend—me—and they team up to catch the Seaside Strangler."

John stared across the bar for a few seconds. "That's actually a great idea, but if we're in Jensen Beach, how do we reunite the original cast?"

"I'll let you work that out."

"Sorry I'm late," said Jessica, stepping up into the bar. She walked up beside John and kissed him on the cheek. "Hey babe."

"Hey," John said.

"Where's my kiss?" Kurt asked.

Jessica leaned over and gave Kurt a kiss on the cheek.

"Thanks," Kurt said. "John invited me to join the two of you for dinner."

"He did, did he?"

"Yeah, and I'm hoping he's paying."

"He isn't," said John.

Violet pointed to her right. "You guys can grab that booth over there and I'll bring some menus over."

"Sounds good," said Kurt. He hopped off the stool and headed for the booth.

"I hope you don't mind," John whispered. "He kind of invited himself."

"I don't mind," Jessica assured him. "It's not like Mulligan's is anything romantic."

John looked around the bar. "Huh," he joked. "You don't think this is romantic?"

"Not at all."

"Maybe you're just too picky."

"Can't be," said Violet. "She's dating you."

"Wow," said John, "that kid of yours is evil, and has a smart mouth."

"Apple doesn't fall far from the tree," Jessica said.

John and Jessica walked to the booth. Jessica slid in first, and John scooted in next to her.

"Do you guys want water?" Violet asked, tossing three menus on the table.

"Yes, please," Jessica replied.

John and Kurt turned down the offer.

When Violet walked away, Jessica asked, "So, how's the case going? Did you find out who the lady is that's supposed to die?"

"Nope," Kurt said, "but we think the *guy* who died may have been run over deliberately."

"Run over?" Jessica asked. She looked at John. "I thought you told me the guy died from cancer, or something, with his family at his side."

"*Loving* family," Kurt said. "But that was the wrong guy."

"Wrong guy?"

"Yeah, Cassie came over to John's with another newspaper she got from Rosie. In it was the obituary of a guy named Mark Steuben. Rosie said that's the guy she dreamed about, not Elliott Guston."

"How does she know that?"

"Because when she saw Steuben's name, she remembered hearing it in her dream."

"That's crazy."

"That's what I've been saying all along," said John, as he scanned his menu.

"She still doesn't remember the name of the next woman who's supposed to die?" Jessica asked.

"No," said Kurt.

"What makes you guys think Steuben was run down on purpose?"

"*You guys* don't think that," said John. "Just he does."

"What makes you think it, Kurt?"

"Just something in my gut. My coply instincts, maybe."

"Brilliant," said John. "Only, you're not a cop."

"I can still have coply instincts," Kurt argued.

"No, you can't."

"Leave him alone, John," Jessica scolded. "He can have coply instincts if he wants."

"Thanks, Jess," Kurt said.

"What about the woman who died first?" asked Jessica.

"We—I mean, *I*—think she may have been pushed down her stairs."

"Huh."

"Have you decided what you want to eat?" Violet asked. She placed a margarita in front of her mother.

"Thanks, sweetheart."

"I'm gonna have the Fried Grouper Rachael," said John, "and just bring something coply for Kurt." John laughed at his own joke. The other three just stared at him. "Ya get it? Like his coply instincts."

"We get it," Jessica said. "It's not funny to pick on people."

"Yeah, John," said Kurt, with a big grin. "It's not funny to pick on people."

"*And*," said Jessica, glaring at her boyfriend, "when was Cassie at your house again to bring you that latest obituary?"

"This morning," Kurt replied for John.

"What, is she there every day now?"

"No, she's not there every day now," John shot back. "She just stopped over to bring us the obits to help with the case."

"She must be a big help to you guys," Jessica said cynically.

"She just drank a quick beer and left," said Kurt.

"Oh, she had a beer?"

John glared at Kurt. "Yes, she had one beer."

"There," said Kurt. "Doesn't it feel better to get the whole truth out?"

"I wasn't lying about anything," said John.

"Let me out," said Jessica, "I have to use the ladies room."

John slid out of the booth and Jessica headed for the restrooms.

"I'll be back over to take your order when she gets back," said Violet. She turned and walked back to the bar.

"Why do you gotta do that?" John asked.

"Do what?" Kurt asked.

"You didn't need to tell her Cassie had a beer."

"And you didn't need to make fun of me about my coply instincts, yet here we are."

"Brilliant."

"Besides, I thought you didn't want to start off a new relationship with lies."

"Not telling her Cassie had a beer isn't a lie. I also didn't say Cole was there. Is that a lie?"

"No, because Cole's a guy."

"Just don't volunteer so much information next time."

When Jessica returned from the ladies' room, she had gotten over Cassie having a beer at John's house. As usual, her unwarranted jealousy—from John's point of view, anyway—was mercifully short-lived. Violet walked back to the table when she saw her mom sitting down, and took the trio's order.

"How'd everything go in there?" Kurt asked.

"In where?" asked Jessica.

"The ladies' room."

"Fine. Why?"

Kurt shrugged. "I don't know."

Jessica sipped her margarita. "So, what exactly does this woman think is happening to her?" she asked. "I mean, does she think she's hearing voices … does she think angels are coming to her in her sleep?"

"She said it was a guy," Kurt pointed out. "So, it can't be angels."

"Aren't all angels guys?" said Jessica.

"Are they?" Kurt said.

"The angel on top of my Christmas tree was always a woman," John offered.

"Was it?" Jessica asked.

"Well, I never looked under her dress."

"Now that I think about it," Kurt recalled, "most of the angels on TV and movies are dudes. There's Clarence, on *It's a Wonderful Life*."

"Nick Cage in *City of Angels*," John added.

"*Nick* Cage?" said Kurt.

"That's his name."

"I think it's *Nicholas* Cage."

"Well, when I lived in Malibu—"

"Here we go," Kurt groaned. "Let's hear about Hollywood and how you were on a first name basis with *Nick* Cage."

"But I—"

Just then Kurt's cell phone rang. "Hold that thought, or better yet, let it go. Hello? Oh, hi, Rosie. Why are you whispering?"

"I don't want Abel to hear me."

"Who's Abel?"

"My boyfriend."

"What's the matter, Rosie?"

"Everything okay?" John asked.

Kurt pressed a bony finger to his lips.

"I'm in the bathroom. Abel's really mad, and he's been drinking. I'm scared."

"Who are you talking to in there?" Kurt heard a man yell. Then he heard pounding.

"Stay where you are, Rosie," said Kurt. "I'll be right there."

"Don't hang up!" Rosie pleaded.

"I won't."

Kurt scooted out of his seat. "Rosie's in trouble," he said.

"Boyfriend?" John asked.

"Yeah."

John looked to Jessica. "I have to go."

"Just go," said Jessica. "Hurry."

John and Kurt headed for the door.

John jumped behind the wheel of his Jeep and Kurt climbed into the passenger seat.

"We're on our way," Kurt said.

"Hurry!" Rosie said.

There was more pounding, and then Kurt heard what he knew was the door being kicked open. The phone went dead.

"Hello?" said Kurt. "Hello? Son of a bitch!"

Chapter Eight

It took John and Kurt about ten minutes to make the trip from Mulligan's to Rosie's place. As the two men got out of the Jeep, they saw a man standing on the front porch of the bungalow that housed her apartment.

Muscular but not bulky, the thirty-something wore dark running pants, a black tank top, and black socks.

"Looks like a ninja wannabe," Kurt mumbled to John. Probably a big pussy." He pointed at the man and said menacingly, "You Abel?"

"No," the guy answered, shaking his head.

"You're not Rosie's boyfriend?" Kurt pressed.

"The girl upstairs? No. That's why I came out here. Something's going on upstairs; I was just about to head up there. You friends of hers?"

"Yeah," John said.

The three men heard a man holler, and then a scream that came from Rosie.

"Shit," Kurt said, and ran across the yard and up the stairs to the second floor. John and the other fella were right behind him.

"Rosie!" Kurt shouted. He tried the doorknob; it was locked.

"Stand back," said the stranger.

Kurt did as he was told, and the stranger slammed his shoulder into the door, busting it open. The three men bolted into the apartment.

Rosie was on her back on the living room floor, with Abel astride her, raining blows down upon her face and torso. Rosie's flailing hands and arms were already heavily bruised from the deflected blows. Abel had drawn back his fist just as the door swung open and slammed against the wall. He froze, and jerked his head toward the trio.

"What the hell do you want?" Abel hollered. "Get out!"

"Help me!" Rosie screamed.

"Get off her!" the stranger ordered.

"Screw you!" said Abel. "Get out of here and mind your own damn business."

Kurt moved toward Abel. The stranger raised his forearm and halted Kurt.

"I got this."

"Oh, you got this, tough guy?" Abel snorted. He gave Rosie one last kick to her ribs with the side of his work boot, and then turned to face the stranger. He put up his fists. "Let's see what you got, tough guy." Abel cracked his neck and the knuckles of both hands.

"If he fights as good as he cracks, this guy's in trouble," Kurt whispered out of the corner of his mouth.

Abel moved around the room, sizing up his opponent. Both men were about the same height, build, and weight. Neither seemed intimidated by the other. The stranger didn't move a muscle as Able slowly circled him.

"You gonna put up your hands, asshole?" Abel asked.

"I don't need to," said the stranger. "But I am going to count to five, and if you haven't made the first move, I will. One."

Abel chuckled. "You're really gonna count."

"Two."

"You expect me to wait till you get to five?"

"Three."

"Counting's pretty scary," Abel ribbed. "You believe this guy?"

"Four."

With lightning speed the stranger karate-chopped Abel in the throat with his left hand and sent his right fist into his gut. As Able doubled over, he brought up his right knee, smashing his nose. Abel's feet came out from under him, and he hit the floor on his back. The floor shook when he hit. Abel wasn't quick enough to block any of it.

John and Kurt looked at each other.

"Holy crap!" Kurt said. "Did you see that?"

"Barely," John replied.

"Maybe he really is a ninja," Kurt added jealously.

The stranger stood over Abel, looking down at his bloody face. "Five," he said.

Abel groaned and felt his nose.

"Rosie?" the stranger asked.

"Yes?"

"Do you ever want to see this gentleman again?"

"No."

The stranger dropped his knee on Abel's chest, and leaned down within inches of the man's ear.

Abel moaned as the air escaped his lungs under the stranger's weight.

"Did you hear her?" the stranger whispered. "She doesn't ever want to see you again."

Abel nodded.

"Say it," said the stranger. "I can't hear the shit in your head slosh around."

"Yes," Abel groaned.

"I live right downstairs. I see you around here again, it'll be your last day on this side of the dirt. You got it?"

"Yes."

The stranger took his knee off Abel's chest and stood. He held out his hand to help Abel up. Abel didn't except the gesture and climbed to his feet on his own.

"Is there anything in this apartment that's yours?" asked the stranger. "Take it now, because you aren't coming back for it."

Abel shook his head.

"What was that?" the stranger demanded.

"No," said Abel.

As Abel walked past Kurt and John on his way to the door, Kurt gave him a swift kick in the ass.

"And stay out," Kurt said.

Abel broke stride just long enough to glower at him before exiting through the doorway. They heard his cowardly taunts from the safety of the stairs, and then the sound of his car cranking and speeding away.

The stranger bent down and helped Rosie to her feet. The young woman stared into his eyes.

"Thank you," she said.

"I'll fix that door first thing tomorrow morning, Rosie," said the stranger. With his fingertips he pushed the hair out of Rosie's eyes. "Are you going to be okay?"

Rosie nodded. Her lips parted.

"He can't hear that," said Kurt. The stranger silenced him with a glance.

"Yes," Rosie said.

The stranger helped Rosie to her sofa. She sat down and thanked him again.

"I guess we don't get a thanks," said Kurt.

"We didn't do anything," John reminded him.

"I'll be right downstairs if you need anything."

"Who *was* that masked man?" Kurt asked. "We didn't even get his name."

John gave his pal a look.

"Oh, sorry," said the stranger. "I'm Charlie Hewitt."

"I'm Rosie."

"I know." Charlie stood and faced John and Kurt. "Charlie Hewitt," he repeated, reaching out to shake.

The three men shook hands and John and Kurt introduced themselves. Before they walked back downstairs, they asked Rosie if there was anyone they could call for her; she told them no, and that she would be fine.

Once back out front of the bungalow, Charlie said, "Don't worry guys, I'm here all day most days. I'll keep an eye on her."

"Thanks," John said.

"How long have you lived in the building?" Kurt asked.

"I just moved in a few weeks ago—the first of the month," Charlie replied.

"Oh," Kurt said. "Move here for work?"

"Yes."

"What is it you do?" John asked.

"I'm a writer."

"Oh, nice. Have you written anything we might have read?"

Charlie grinned. "Well, that all depends. Have you read any of the Martin County Mysteries?"

"I don't think so. What pen name do you use?"

"I use my own name."

"Sorry, I've never heard of them."

"That's okay. I get that a lot."

"So, you're in town doing research?" Kurt asked.

"Kind of," said Charlie. "More of a tax-deductible vacation really."

"I see," said John.

"How long are you in town?" Kurt asked.

"Until the end of next month."

Kurt took out his wallet, being careful not to let Charlie see the plastic police badge. "Here," he said, "let me give you my cell phone number."

"Put that away," said John. "I'll give him my number."

Kurt shrugged it off and put the wallet back in his pocket.

John rattled off his cell phone number and Charlie entered it into his contacts. Charlie then sent John a quick text so he would have his number.

The three men said their goodbyes, and John and Kurt hopped back into the Jeep and drove away.

"We were lucky Charlie was there," John said.

"I'm sure we would have done just fine without him," Kurt responded.

"Are you kidding me? Did you see how fast that guy's hands were?"

"I think I could have taken Abel."

"Maybe."

"Maybe? The guy got beat up by writer, for Chrissakes. Charlie got in a couple lucky hits. Not to mention, they were cheap shots."

"Why do you say that?"

"He said he was gonna count to five, but he only counted to four. He caught Abel off guard."

"I don't get you. Charlie's just the kind of guy you would usually be impressed with."

"Well, I'm not."

"Why not? Oh, because you're jealous."

"Jealous of what?" Kurt shot back. "Why would I be jealous of *him*."

"Did you see the way Rosie looked at him when he pulled her to her feet?"

"Shut up."

"I think it was love at first sight."

"Seriously, enough."

"I guess Charlie didn't remind Rosie of her father."

"Just get me back to Mulligan's. I'm hungry and I need a drink."

"Maybe Bonnie's working tonight. That'll cheer you up."

"Maybe."

"You know what we should do? We should invite Charlie to Mulligan's for a drink."

"No! We shouldn't."

Chapter Nine

Jessica was seated at the bar when John and Kurt returned to Mulligan's.

"I put your meals in to-go containers," Violet told them. "They're back in the kitchen."

"Thanks, Violet," said Kurt. "You're awesome."

"I know."

John kissed Jessica on the cheek and sat down on the stool to her left. "Sorry about running out on you like that," he said.

"Don't worry about it," Jessica said. "How'd everything go? Did you save the day?"

"I wouldn't say we saved the day."

"Kurt took the stool to Jessica's right. "You can heat that back up for me now," Kurt said.

"Oh, can I?" Violet shot back. She was preparing a strawberry daiquiri for another customer. "I'll get right on it."

"Thanks, and I'll also have a Jack and Coke."

"I'll put you on the list."

"What do you mean, you didn't save the day?" Jessica asked.

"We had a little help," John explained.

"But we could have done it ourselves," Kurt put in.

"Done what yourselves?" Jessica asked.

"Rosie's boyfriend showed up," Kurt said, "and he was slapping her around. Had her on the floor when we busted the door in."

"When *we* busted the door in?" said John.

"When Charlie busted the door in," Kurt said.

"Who's Charlie?" asked Jessica.

"John's new friend," Kurt replied sulkily.

"He rents the apartment downstairs from Rosie," John said. "He was standing out on the front porch when we arrived. He heard the fighting going on upstairs and was on his way up."

"And he kicked in Rosie's door?" Jessica said.

"He threw his shoulder into it," said John. "And then he kicked the crap out of Abel—that's Rosie's boyfriend."

"No kidding?"

"Yeah, it was crazy. He had Abel on his back in, like, a second. Never seen anyone's hands move that fast."

"Blah, blah, blah," said Kurt. "I could have done the same thing."

"Maybe the result would have been the same," said John, "but it wouldn't have been that fast."

"Slow and steady wins the race," said Kurt.

"Only in nursery rhymes," said Violet. She placed Kurt's Jack and Coke in front of him.

"The Tortoise and the Hare wasn't a nursery rhyme; it was a fable."

"Isn't *fable* another word for lie?"

"Yeah, and *shut it* is another word for be quiet."

"That's two words. What can I get you, John?"

"That Jack and Coke sounds good," John answered.

"Comin' right up."

"You ever hear of Charlie Hewitt?" John asked.

"Should I have?" asked Jessica.

"He's a writer."

"What's he write?"

"The Martin County Mysteries."

"Never heard of him."

"Me neither," Kurt said.

"Do you read?" Jessica asked.

"Magazines, and sometimes the newspaper. Never was much of a book reader."

"Ya wouldn't know it," Violet deadpanned.

"Is it just me," Kurt asked, "or have you guys been picking on me a lot in the last few days?"

"It's just you," said Violet. She grabbed her cell phone off the back bar and began tapping the screen.

Kurt leaned forward and looked past Jessica at John. "Remember those damn book reports we had to do for Mr. Wallace?" he asked.

John shook his head. "Hated those. One book report per month, and every other one was oral."

"I never did the oral ones. Wallace would call on me, and I'd say, 'didn't do it,' and it was a big fat zero."

"Failed English that year, didn't you?"

"Sure did. Eight weeks of summer school, and I would have failed that too, if it wasn't for your mom helping me with my homework every night … and feeding me … and everything else she did for me."

"You must have spent a lot of time at John's when you were a kid," said Jessica.

"As much time as I could." Kurt picked up his glass and sipped his drink. "I loved it over there. John's family was like the Waltons, but with only two kids."

Jessica reached over and rubbed John's back. "I guess that makes you John Boy."

"It sure does," said John.

"So, were you going to heat up those meals for us?" Kurt hinted.

"Hold on," said Violet. "Here he is."

"Here who is?" Kurt asked.

"Charlie Hewitt. Wow, he's cute."

"Let me see," said Jessica.

"Says here on his Amazon page that he's written eleven books," Violet reported. "They're available in Kindle, paperback, and Audible. He also writes a series that takes place in California, and one in Texas."

"Let me see that," said Kurt, snatching the cell from her. He read aloud: "'Charlie Hewitt is an American crime and suspense novelist. Charlie was born and raised in Kenton, Ohio, and is best known for his Martin County Mystery Series.'" Kurt rolled his eyes. "Best known by who?"

"How much are the e-books?" John asked.

"What the hell's an e-book?" Kurt asked.

"The Kindle."

"Oh." Kurt scrolled through the book list. "Four ninety-nine."

"Can I have my phone back?" Violet asked.

"Can you even make a living selling books for five bucks?" Kurt asked, handing Violet her cell phone.

"All depends on how many he sells," John answered.

"Says here his last book came out six months ago," Violet shared, "and it's 2,302—number sixty-one in the private detective category." she scrolled down Charlie's author page. "His first book came out six years ago, and it's still doing pretty well."

"Sounds like he makes a pretty good living," said John.

"I doubt there's been any movies made based on his books. The screenplay we're writing probably will be," Kurt boasted.

"*We're* writing?" John questioned.

"I've got some ideas," Kurt said angrily.

"Well, let's see them."

"Next week."

"It's a date."

"How old is he?" Violet asked, staring at Charlie's photograph.

"I don't know," John replied. "Early thirties, maybe."

"He's so cute," Violet repeated, holding the cell phone so her mom could see it.

"Very handsome," Jessica agreed.

"He's too young for your mother," said John.

"What's that supposed to mean?" asked Jessica.

John knew instantly he had stuck his foot in his mouth. "I meant immature," he backpedaled. "He seems like a kid, and you're—"

"Old?"

"No. Mature."

"Nice try," said Kurt, chuckling.

John leaned over for a kiss, but was rejected.

"I'm really getting hungry," said Kurt.

"Oh, yeah," said Violet. She walked from behind the bar and made her way to the kitchen.

Kurt turned to Jessica. "Well, I think you look very young," he said.

"I am young!" said Jessica.

"I thought you were my age?"

"I am!"

"Oh."

"Nice try," said John.

"No kiss for you either," Jessica said.

Chapter Ten

Sunday around noon John and Kurt hopped in John's Jeep and headed for Conner Cady's house. Before making the trip, they decided it would be a better idea to act as though they were investigating Mark Steuben's death, and not Vicky's.

John looked over to see his friend fussing with his wallet again. "What are you doing now?" he asked.

"Taking out this badge and exchanging the fake detective ID for my fake private investigator ID," Kurt replied.

"Seriously?"

"Yeah, I know, it's stupid. I should have just gotten two wallets."

"Yeah, that's what's stupid about it."

Kurt turned in the passenger seat and faced John. He flipped open the wallet. "Dirk Stone—PI," he announced.

"Good God."

"Does it look real?"

"I guess. I don't know if I've ever seen a private investigator's license."

"Take my word for it, it looks real. I printed it—"

"Off your computer. I know."

John pulled his Jeep to the curb in front of a two-story house on Wycoff Street, in Port Saint Lucie. The tan stucco home appeared to be the only two-story place on the block. Two vehicles were parked side by side in the driveway—a black Ford F-150, and a yellow Volkswagen Bug.

"That's some shitty luck," Kurt observed.

"What do you mean?" John asked.

"If they had bought any other house on the street, Vicky Cady would still be alive. One good thing about a ranch-style home: you can't tumble down the stairs to your death."

"Make sure you mention that to her husband," John said sarcastically.

"Unless …"

"Unless what?"

"Unless she was murdered. The killer would have just found a different way to kill her."

"Like run over her with a car."

"Exactly!"

"Yeah, exactly."

The two men climbed out of the Jeep.

"I'm guessing the yellow Bug is Vicky's," Kurt surmised.

"That would be my guess," John agreed.

"Time to do some lying."

They walked up the driveway. Conner Cady answered Kurt's knock on the door.

"Can I help you?" he asked.

Kurt flashed his ID. "Good morning, sir," he said. "My name is Dirk Stone. I'm a private investigator working for the family of Mark Steuben. This is my associate, Brock Storm."

Conner appeared confused. "Mark Steuben?" He tried to get a closer look at the ID, but Kurt flipped it closed too quickly.

"Yes, we were wondering if we could ask you a few questions."

"I don't understand. Who's Mark Steuben? Questions about what?"

"Mr. Steuben was killed in a hit-and-run a few days ago," John clarified. "We're working for the Steuben family, trying to identify the driver of the vehicle."

"What does this have to do with me?" Conner demanded.

"More your wife than you," Kurt said.

Conner folded his arms across his chest. "What the hell's this got to do with Vicky?"

John spoke up. "Her Volkswagen Bug was seen on security footage at a local running trail—Woodstork Trail, around Hillmoor Lake."

"It was the same day Mark Steuben was also running on the trail," Kurt explained. "Another witness said they saw Mr. Steuben get into an altercation with a man in the parking lot."

"It was the day before the hit-and-run," John said.

"I see," Conner said softly.

"Would it be possible to ask your wife a couple questions?" Kurt asked. "I see her Bug is parked in the driveway."

Conner took a deep breath. "I'm afraid that would be impossible," he said, eyes watering. "My wife passed away last week."

Kurt and John exchanged feigned looks of surprise.

"Passed away?" Kurt asked.

"May we ask how?" said John.

"She slipped and fell down the stairs."

"Oh, my God. I'm so sorry. We had no idea."

"Very sorry for your loss, Mr. Cady," Kurt said.

Conner nodded. "Thank you."

"Was she home alone when it happened?" Kurt asked.

"Yes. I was at work. Our daughter Lauren found her lying at the bottom of the stairs."

"That must have been terrible for her," John said.

"It was."

"Mr. Cady, I have to ask: did your wife know Mark Steuben?"

Conner gave a slight shrug. "Not that I know of. I've never heard her mention the name."

"Thank you for your time, Mr. Cady." Kurt removed his wallet, and took out one of his business cards. "If you think of anything else, please don't hesitate to give me a call."

"Think of anything like what?"

"Maybe your daughter or one of your wife's friends remembers her speaking of Mr. Steuben. You might bring it up casually in conversation."

Conner nodded. "Okay, but I'm sure I would have known if my wife and this Steuben guy were friends. I know all of her friends."

"I'm sure you would have," said Kurt. "Thanks again for your time."

Kurt and John walked back down the driveway and got back into John's Wrangler. As they pulled away from the curb Kurt noticed Conner still in the doorway holding his business card.

"I don't think that could have gone any better," said Kurt.

"Except for the fact that now Cady is wondering if his wife had a male friend he didn't know about."

"Yeah, there's that, but I'm sure she didn't, so nothing for us to worry about."

"No, but something for him to worry about."

"Ya gotta admit though, that was a pretty good story we came up with about her car being spotted at the running trail."

"Yeah, pretty good. We're just lucky he didn't ask what day it was."

"I would have just said a day. With the grief he's been through in the last week or so, he wouldn't remember what day she ran and what day she didn't."

"You're probably right."

"What's next?"

"You tell me."

"I have no idea where to go from here. If Vicky Cady and Mark Steuben didn't know each other, we have no way of knowing if their deaths are connected."

"I don't think they were. Cady fell down the stairs, and Steuben got hit by a car. Simple as that."

"Only it's not as simple as that, because someone dreamed about their deaths before they happened."

"Or did she? Maybe Rosie's just a young girl with a big imagination who's looking for attention."

"Maybe."

"I think this is a wild goose chase."

"We'll know in a few days."

"Why do you say that?"

"Because, if Rosie is right, the Grim Reaper comes calling again on Wednesday."

"Well, let's just hope she's wrong."

"Speaking of Rosie, let's run by her place and make sure her door got fixed."

"You don't think Charlie fixed it?"

"I just want to make sure he did."

"You got it." John hung a right off Becker Road onto Citrus Boulevard.

Kurt reached down and turned on the radio. Jon Pardi was singing "Heartache Medication." He scowled at John and asked, "What's this crap?"

"What, you don't like country?"

"No."

Kurt quickly tuned it to 98.7 The Shark, where Jim Morrison was belting out "Twentieth Century Fox." Kurt started headbanging and playing air guitar.

"I had a meeting at 20th Century Fox once," John reminisced. "I was up for the male lead in *Night at the Museum*."

"No shit. That's awesome," Kurt said with admiration. "How did it go?"

"Well, I'm driving around Florida with you in a used Jeep, and I haven't worked in months."

"Enough said, pal."

Chapter Eleven

John was sitting by himself in one of the lounge chairs alongside his pool Wednesday evening a little before five. Half a bottle of LandShark sat on the plastic table next to him. He was on his cell phone.

"It's a paycheck, John. What do you want me to tell you?"

"You're my manager, Dave. I want you to tell me that I don't have to do anymore personal appearances. I want you to tell me that you have a movie or a pilot for me."

"So, you want me to lie to you?"

"That's not funny."

"I know, Johnny Boy, but—"

"I've asked you not to call me that, Dave."

"Sorry, John, it's a habit."

"Break it, please."

"The appearances get you out there," David Lutz explained. "You don't want people to forget about you, do you?"

"No."

"Something will come up, John, I promise."

"That's what you said last month when I talked to you, and the month before."

"This kind of thing happens sometimes. One minute you're on top of the world, next minute, you're nobody."

"I'm nobody now?"

"That's not what I meant."

"It's what you said. And what do you mean, this happens sometimes. To who? Name someone else."

"Brendan Fraser, Jonathan Taylor Thomas, Bridget Fonda, Freddie Prinze Jr., Amanda—"

"Okay, okay, I get it. But every one of those actors you named is worth at least ten mil, and they're all still working to some extent, as forgettable as that work may be. I'm worth less than three mil, and it isn't going to last very long if I don't get something. I've got child support to pay."

"That's why you have to take these appearances, John. It keeps your name out there, and it pays a little. Also, I spoke with Sal. He says—"

"Why the hell are you speaking with my accountant?"

"He's worried about you, John. He says you just put in a pool with a waterfall for fifty-one grand?"

"Uh … yeah."

"Maybe that's not such a good idea at the moment."

"I bought a used Jeep."

"For thirty eight-grand."

"Is Sal supposed to be telling you how much I spend? I don't think he is."

"Just lay off the spending for a while. At least until we get you working again."

"When will that be?"

"Soon."

"Yeah, soon—oh, there was something I wanted to ask you about."

"What's that?"

"Has there ever been any talk of a *Law of the Land* reunion?"

Dave chuckled. "Reunion? You mean like they did with *Roseanne* and *Will and Grace?*"

"Yeah. Why are you laughing?"

"I was coughing."

"Sounded like a chuckle."

"Your show didn't have the following those shows had."

"I'm on Netflix and Hulu."

"Everyone is on Netflix and Hulu." Dave sighed. "I might as well tell you."

"Tell me what?"

"There's been some chatter about a *Law of the Land* movie. Michael Bay has shown some interest."

"Oh my God! That's great, Dave!"

"Michael B. Jordan is on the short list to play Mason Land."

"Wait—what? But *I'm* Mason Land."

"You *were* Mason Land."

"Michael B. Jordan is black."

"Yes. Your point?"

"Mason Land is white."

"No, John, the actor who played Mason Land is white. The character can be any color the writer wants him to be. Magnum P.I. is Mexican-American now. Dr. Who is a woman. Hey, maybe we can get you a cameo. The old Mason Land meets the new Mason Land"

"You mean, I'll be like David Soul and Paul Michael Glaser in that *Starsky & Hutch* movie."

"Exactly."

"I spent fifty-one thousand dollars on a pool to drown myself. I could have gotten a gun so much cheaper."

"Cheer up, John. Something will come along. How's the screenplay on the what's-his-name—the Seaside Strangler—coming?"

"Good."

"How much have you written? I'd like to read it, maybe shop it around."

"I'm on page four."

"Page four? In six weeks?"

"I haven't been that motivated lately."

"Maybe when you're living in a cardboard box you'll be more motivated." Dave laughed out loud.

"Wow, you're a real comedian today."

"I'm sorry, Johnny Boy. Hang in there. Gotta go, I got someone on the other line."

"Who?"

"You don't know him."

"Who is it, Dave?"

"Michael B. Jordan."

"You bastard."

John hung up his cell phone, checked the time, and tossed it on the table next to his beer bottle. He picked up the beer and chugged it. "One of these ain't gonna do it," he said. *I do need a refrigerator out here.*

The beleaguered actor climbed defeatedly out of his lounge chair and headed inside for another beer. As he opened the fridge, he noticed he'd left the television on in the living room. He twisted off the cap and walked into the room. He stared at TV screen as lovely WPTV anchor Kelley Dunn reported on the shooting that had occurred that morning.

"The female victim, whose name is being withheld pending notification of next of kin, was the manager of the Seagull Motel on Peters Road in Fort Pierce. She was walking across the parking lot from her car to the motel office when an unknown assailant shot her point-blank in the back of the head. The victim was pronounced dead at the scene. The investigation is ongoing. We'll have more on this developing story on our eleven o'clock broadcast."

John had a strange feeling in the pit of his stomach as he hurried poolside and grabbed his cell.

"Hey, Kurt. You watching the news?"

"No, why? I'm at the store. What's going on?"

"Maybe it's nothing. I'll be right there."

"Is it the third victim, John?"

"I'm not sure."

"Did you hear from Rosie?"

"No. I'll be right there."

Chapter Twelve

Kurt was standing on the sidewalk out front of the Pineapple Surf Shop when John rolled up in his Jeep. He was dressed in a pair of board shorts and a red tank top that said LIFEGUARD on the front.

"What's going on?" Kurt asked.

A tourist walking by answered, "Not much."

"I wasn't talking to you," said Kurt. "Move along."

The guy gave Kurt a dirty look.

"Did you hear about the woman who was shot in Fort Pierce this morning?" John asked.

"Nope. Been stuck here all day."

Kurt was within earshot of Sara Burkowska, his only full-time employee. She rolled her eyes at his comment.

"Yeah," Sara said, "the poor thing. He's been stuck in his own store all day … for once."

Kurt waved her off, grabbed the doorknob, and pulled the door closed behind him.

"Real mature, Kurt!" Sara hollered.

John walked around the front of his Jeep and met Kurt on the sidewalk.

"So what's going on?' Kurt asked.

"I'm not sure," John replied. "I just had this funny feeling when I saw the news."

"What did you see on the news?" Kurt asked impatiently.

"A woman was shot in the head on her way across the parking lot at the Seagull Motel in Fort Pierce."

"You think it's our third victim?"

"I don't know. You have Rosie's phone number?"

"Yeah." Kurt reached into his side pocket and pulled out his cell phone.

"Just give her a call and ask her if she saw the news."

"I have two missed calls from her," said Kurt, gazing at his screen.

"Crap."

Kurt tapped the cell screen a couple times and put the phone to his ear. "Hey, Rosie. You called?"

"Yes, Kurt. Why didn't you answer?" she asked frantically.

"My ringer was off. What's the matter?"

"A woman was shot to death in Fort Pierce this morning."

"I heard. Is it her?"

"I think it is."

"What makes you think it is?"

"I'm not sure, but I think I remember something about a motel from my dream."

"Okay. Calm down. We'll look into it and I'll get back to you."

"What should I do in the meantime?"

"Nothing. You working tonight?"

"No, I have tonight off. I don't want to sit here alone. I'm kinda scared now."

"You want me to come over?"

"Hold on. Someone's knocking at the door. Should I answer it?"

"Yeah, go ahead."

"Oh, it's just Charlie. Hold on a second, Kurt."

John was waiting for answers. "What's going on? Is she—"

"Shhh," said Kurt, straining to hear Rosie and Charlie's conversation.

"Hey, Charlie. What's up?"

"I was running to the grocery store," Charlie said, "and I figured I'd run up and see if you needed me to pick anything up for you."

"Oh, that's so sweet. I do need a few things."

Kurt rolled his eyes.

"Better yet," Charlie said, "would you rather go to the store with me?"

"That would be great. I'd love to get out of the house." Rosie put her cell phone back up to her ear. "Hey, Kurt?"

"Yeah?"

"Everything's fine. I'm gonna run to the grocery store with Charlie."

"Uh, yeah, sounds good. Talk to you later."

Kurt hung up and slid his cell back into his pocket.

"Well?" John asked.

"She thinks the woman who was killed this morning is the person she dreamed about, because she remembers something about a motel from her dream."

"I heard you ask Rosie if she wanted you to come over. Is she okay?"

"She's fine now. Sir Galahad showed up to save the day."

"Sir Galahad?"

"Charlie Hewitt, writer extraordinaire."

John chuckled. "Jealous?"

"No."

"Whatever you say. Come on, let's go."

"Where?"

"To the Breakwater Bar and Grill. We'll see if Cole can find out exactly what happened at the Seagull Motel."

"I'm sure he can, but will he share that information with us?"

"Let's hope so."

Kurt pushed the door open. "Hey, Sara, I'm leaving for a couple hours."

"A couple hours?" Sara sneered. "So, I'll see you tomorrow?"

"I might be back tonight."

"I'll see you tomorrow. Take care of him, John."

"I will," John replied.

The crime-fighting duo hopped into John's Jeep and sped off.

"Sara told me to take care of you," John said.

"Yeah, so?"

"She seems to really like you."

"What makes you say that?"

"Just the way she looks at you, and talks to you. The two of you seem like a couple."

"We're not."

"I know. Why not?"

"Why not what?"

"Why aren't you a couple?"

"I don't know."

"You ever ask her out?"

"No! Why would I do that?"

"You ask everyone else out. Why don't you ask her out?"

"Because … she's Sara."

"What's that supposed to mean?"

"She's like family … like a friend. She worked for my dad since she was a kid."

"You were a kid then too, Kurt," John pointed out. "You were never interested? I think she's kind of cute."

"Then you ask her out."

"I mean, I think she's kind of cute for you."

"She's not my type."

"What type is she?"

"Tall, thin, and long, curly hair."

"You're tall, thin, and have long, curly hair."

"Exactly. It would be like dating myself."

"You should be used to that," John said, laughing. "When are you and your right hand going to get married."

"Very funny."

Chapter Thirteen

When John and Kurt entered the Breakwater, Cole's daughter, Allison, was standing behind the bar. She had her foot up on the bar sink and was leaning over the bar eating French fries off of a young man's plate. The young man sitting on the stool across from her was dressed in a conservative tan suit. His short light hair was combed neatly to the side. He had clear skin and perfect teeth and posture that would do Emily Post proud. He looked like every Mormon kid John had ever seen.

"Hey, guys," Allison said, when she saw the two men enter.

"Hey Allison," Kurt said.

"Oh my gosh!" said Allison's friend. His jaw dropped. "You're John Burton!"

John smiled. It was still nice to be recognized.

"I am," he replied. "And you are?" John held out his hand to shake.

"I'm John Burton—I mean, I'm Spence Oller. You're John Burton." He swung his leg off the back of the stool and shook John's hand.

John grinned big. It had been a long time since he had caused a tongue to be tied. "It's nice to meet you, Spence."

"Spence is my boyfriend, John," Allison explained. "He's a detective with the Fort Pierce Police Department."

"Ya don't say."

Spence shot Allison an inquisitive look. "How do you know John Burton?"

"He's a friend of my dad's," Allison said. "He's been in here a few times."

Spence shook his head like he was trying to awaken from a dream. "Holy cow! Your father is a friend of John Burton's? How it is that no one's ever mentioned this to me?" His eyes were as huge as SpongeBob SquarePants gazing adoringly at a Krabby Patty.

"Calm down, kid," said Cole. He walked from the kitchen toward the group. "I just met him myself a few weeks ago. Didn't know you were a fan."

Kurt stepped up beside Spence and offered his hand. "I'm Kurt Powell."

Spence shook Kurt's hand while never taking his eyes off John.

"What brings you to Fort Pierce?" asked Spence eagerly. "Are you working on a movie?"

Cole snorted. John shot him a look.

"No," John said. "I just bought a place in Jensen Beach. I grew up there."

"No kidding? I had no idea."

"His parents still live here," Kurt threw in.

"Wow. Small world. Can I buy you a drink?"

"That would be great, Spence," John said. "Thank you."

"Get him whatever he wants," Spence told Allison. "It's on me."

"What'll it be, John?" Allison asked.

"Jack and Coke," John answered.

"Jack and Coke for me too," said Kurt. He side stepped around John and Spence and swung his leg over one of the stools.

Spence was still grinning. "John Burton, right here in the bar with me. Ya know, I think I was only like ten or eleven years old when your show started. Me and my dad watched it every week. Then sometimes I would see old reruns. As a matter of fact, I binge watched the whole series about a year ago on Netflix." Spence reminisced to himself for a second, and then blurted out: "Crime don't pay, dickhead, but you will!" He gave Allison an apologetic look. "excuse my language, hon. That was Mason Land's catchphrase."

John nodded. "Yep, that was it."

"Loved it. So, what are you working on these days?"

"Not mu—"

"We're writing a screenplay together," Kurt interjected. "All about the Seaside Strangler, and how the two of us caught him."

"Seaside strangler?"

Allison slid Kurt's drink in front of him, and then handed John's to him.

"Yeah, you remember—the guy who murdered those two women a few months back. The cop got shot."

"Oh, yeah. The lady was strangled in Port Saint Lucie, at that hotel, and the other one at those cabins on Indian River Drive," Spence recalled. "I didn't remember hearing it was John Burton who caught the guy."

"And me," said Kurt.

"We let the officer who got shot take most of the credit," John explained. He tipped up his glass and took a drink. "We did get a little award from the city of Stuart."

"And ten grand each from one of the victim's husbands," John added.

"That we gave to charity," Kurt grumbled.

"What was that?" Spence asked.

"We gave the money to charity," Kurt repeated, this time a little more audible and enthusiastic.

"That's really nice of you guys."

"That's what they tell me."

"I also didn't remember the guy being called the Seaside Strangler," said Spence.

"I made that part up," Kurt admitted.

"Ya think someone will make it into a movie, John?" Spence asked.

"We'll see," said John.

"Wow, I just can't believe that a guy who played a cop on TV turned around and caught a real bad guy."

"Which brings us to why we're here," said Kurt.

"Here we go," Cole said. "I was wondering why you boys stopped in."

"It sure wasn't for the atmosphere, the food, or the great prices," mocked the old man at the end of the bar.

"Pipe down, Melvin," Cole shot back. "This conversation is for those of us who aren't a million years old."

"Up yours." The old guy slid his empty glass forward. "Can I get one more princess?"

"Sure, Mr. Mulhern."

John hopped up on a bar stool to Spence's right, keeping the young detective between him and Kurt.

"So, why are you here?" Spence asked.

"There was a woman murdered this morning at the Seagull Motel over on Peters Road," said Kurt.

"Yeah, I know about it." Spence replied. He picked up his plastic tumbler of ginger ale and sipped it. "What about it?"

"Is it your case?"

"No."

"Who has it?" Cole asked.

"I think it's Franklin."

"Is this about the woman who sees the future?" Cole asked.

"She doesn't see the future," said John.

"She just dreams about people who will be murdered," Kurt said.

"Doesn't sound like much of a difference."

John swirled his Jack and Coke, took a sip. "To answer your question, Cole," said John, "yes, we think it's connected."

"How?"

"We don't know, but the young girl who dreamed about the first two deaths told us the woman at the Seagull Motel was the third victim."

"Let me guess, she told you after the woman was killed."

"Yes."

"And did you think to ask her why she thinks this woman is the one she dreamt about?"

"Yes," Kurt answered. "She said after she saw the story on the news, she remembered there was something in her dream about a motel."

"Just like she remembered Steuben's name after she saw the obituary."

"Correct."

"It's not strange to you that she only remembers these things after someone has died?" Cole asked.

"It seems *very* strange," John said.

"But it doesn't mean it's not true," Kurt threw in.

"And it doesn't mean it is," said Cole.

"How well do you know this Detective Franklin?" John asked.

"*Very* well," said Cole.

"We need to find out if this woman is connected to Mark Steuben or Vicky Cady," Kurt said.

"Go ahead and do that," Cole said.

"They're withholding the woman's name until next of kin is notified," said John. "We need that information now."

Spence sat quietly listening and wondering what the hell the three men were talking about.

"The quicker we get her name, the quicker we can figure out if she's connected," Kurt said.

"Did you find out if the other two knew each other?" Cole asked.

"We questioned Vicky Cady's husband," said John. "As far as he knows, she and Steuben didn't know each other."

"Is there a fourth victim?" Allison asked.

Cole smiled big. "Good question, princess," he said.

Spence squinted in confusion. "How do you even know what's going on, Allison?" he asked.

"I've been listening."

"So have I."

"*Is* there a fourth victim?" Cole repeated his daughter's inquiry.

"Not as far as we know," said John.

"Can you give Franklin a call for us, Cole?" Kurt asked.

"Nope."

"Why not?"

"Because it's stupid. No one dreams about upcoming murders. It just doesn't happen. That little bartender is just looking for attention, and she's not getting it from me. I'm not gonna bother Tommy with it."

Kurt turned to Spence. "How about you, Spence?" he asked, all smiles. "Would you be interested in doing one of your favorite actors a favor? Who knows, maybe we could get you a bit part in the Seaside Strangler movie. Maybe we could even get you on as technical advisor."

"Technical advisor? Wow!" Spence looked to Cole for advice.

"Don't look at me, Spence," said Cole. "You're a big boy. You do what you want."

Spence went for his cell phone.

"Thanks, Spence," Kurt said.

Spence tapped his screen a few times and scrolled through his contacts until he came to Tommy Franklin. The detective answered on the first ring.

"What can I do for ya, kid?"

"The woman killed this morning at the Seagull Motel, what was her name?"

"Florence Ivy. Why, what's up?"

"Just curious."

"There must be a reason you're asking."

"It's probably nothing, but I've been working a cold case and—"

"I don't mean to cut you off, kid, but I don't need the long version."

"You asked me."

"Yeah, and regretted it the second I did. Is that it?"

"Any witnesses?"

"Nope. No one saw a thing."

"Okay, thanks, Tommy." Spence hung up the phone. "The woman's name is Florence Ivy."

"Witnesses say what the assailant was driving?" John asked.

"No witnesses."

"Figures," Kurt said. He tipped up his drink and downed the remainder. "Come on, John."

"Let me finish my drink," John protested.

"Hurry up! We need to talk to Vicky Cady's husband again and see if he's ever heard of Florence Ivy."

John groaned. "Fine." He gulped down the rest of his drink and hopped off his stool.

"You guys have fun," Cole said, "and stop back by later for dinner. I'm very interested to hear how it turns out."

"Really?" Kurt asked.

"No," said Cole.

Allison and Melvin Mulhern laughed out loud.

All heads turned toward Melvin as he wheezed and convulsed in the throes of hilarity. His shoulders shook as he chuckled and tried to catch his breath.

"He's turning blue," John pointed out.

"Should we do something?" Kurt asked.

"He'll snap out of it," Cole assured them.

"When?" Kurt asked.

"Soon," said Spence.

Melvin inhaled a long, deep breath. His color returned to its usual corpse-like pallor.

"What're y'all lookin' at?" he groused.

"We thought we lost ya for a second there," Cole said. "but then you disappointed us by coming back to life."

"Up yours, Ballinger."

Chapter Fourteen

Thirty-five minutes later, John and Kurt pulled up in front of Conner Cady's house. Both cars were in the driveway.

The two mock detectives climbed out of the Jeep and walked to the door. Kurt knocked.

Conner Cady was stone-faced when he opened the door. "What can I do for you gentlemen?" he asked, with a note of irritation.

"Mr. Cady, we do apologize for this intrusion in your time of grief," Kurt began. "I'll cut right to the chase—does the name Florence Ivy mean anything to you?"

Conner sighed. "No. Should it?"

"It's in connection with the Mark Steuben hit-and-run," John explained.

"Your wife never mentioned the name Florence Ivy?" Kurt asked.

"Why would she?"

"We're just trying to make a connection between Steuben and Florence Ivy."

"Look, detectives, I've tried my best to be polite and cooperative, but frankly, you're wearing out your welcome and wasting my time. I don't know them, and neither did Vicky."

"Did you ask your children—"

"I'm sorry, Mr. Stone, but as you can imagine, these past couple of weeks have been very difficult on me and my family. So, if you could please just go."

Conner slowly closed the door.

John and Kurt looked at each other.

"Come on, Kurt, let's go."

The sun had set before they arrived, and now the evening sky was growing darker as they walked down the driveway.

"Want to drive back to the Breakwater for something to eat?" Kurt suggested.

"Naw, I don't want to drive all the way back over there. Let's just go to—"

"Psst!"

John looked over at his friend. "Did you spring a leak?"

"That wasn't me," Kurt replied.

"Psst!"

The two men looked to their left, toward the neighbor's house.

"Psst!"

Standing in the darkness between the two houses was a shadowy figure.

"Who's over there?" John asked.

"Shhh! Come here," whispered the figure.

"What do you want?" Kurt whispered back.

"Follow me."

The whisperer turned and walked to the back of the neighbor's house. John checked Conner's windows as he and Kurt walked between the houses, to make sure he wasn't looking out. A patch of moonlight revealed a dark-haired woman in her thirties.

"Who are you?" John demanded, "a what are you doing skulking around out here?"

"I'm not skulking—this is my house. My name is Gigi Myers. I heard you talking to Conner. Are you the cops?"

"Private cops," said Kurt.

"I see. I heard you mention Mark Steuben's name."

"Gigi, what do you know about Mark?" John asked.

"I know he was Vicky's boyfriend."

"How do you know this?"

"Because Vicky was my best friend."

"And she told you she was seeing Mark Steuben?" Kurt asked.

"Yes."

"Is Conner aware of this?"

"Not that I know of," Gigi replied.

"Have you ever met Mark?" John asked.

"No. Never."

"How long had they been seeing each other?" Kurt asked.

"Vicky told me about it two months ago, and at the time, she had been seeing him for six months."

"Do you know if Conner was home the day Vicky took her tumble down the stairs? He said he wasn't; we want to confirm if that's true."

"No, he wasn't home. He was at work. Their daughter stopped over to pick Vicky up and found her at the bottom of the stairs. I was here when Conner came home. He was devastated. Have you spoken with Mark?"

"Mark was killed in a hit-and-run last week," said John.

Gigi's hand went to her mouth. "Oh my goodness! That's terrible. Did the police catch the person who hit him?"

"No."

Gigi thought for a second. "Do you think Vicky's accident *wasn't* an accident?"

"Beginning to look that way," said Kurt. "Have you ever heard the name, Florence Ivy?" asked Kurt.

"Doesn't sound familiar. Why, do you think she's the person who hit Mark?"

Kurt shrugged. "We don't know."

"Did Vicky ever tell you where she and Mark would meet?" John asked.

"Yes. It was some little motel up in Fort Pierce."

"The Seagull Motel?"

"Yeah, that's it."

Kurt reached into his pocket for a business card. "If you think of anything else that might be helpful to us, please give me a call."

Gigi tilted the card in the moonlight to read it. "Detective Dirk Stone?"

Kurt snatched the card out of her hand. "Sorry, wrong one." He grabbed one of the cards that read Dirk Stone Private Investigator and handed it to her. "There ya go. Like I said, give me a call."

"Okay, Mr. Stone, I will."

John and Kurt walked stealthily back to the Jeep and drove away.

"Sorry, wrong one?" said John. "How could you hand her the wrong card, you jack ass?"

Kurt laughed. "I really do need two wallets."

Chapter Fifteen

After listening to what Gigi Myers had told them, John and Kurt decided that maybe it would be a good idea to return the Breakwater Bar and Grill to speak with Cole.

"Do you think we should give Rosie a call and let he know what's going on?" Kurt asked, as John rounded Jetty Park looking for a parking spot. "I mean, after all, she hired us."

"Hired us?" John scoffed. "Hired us would imply that she was paying us."

Kurt nodded. "Yeah, it sure would be nice to get paid for doing this investigation stuff."

John whipped into a space in front of the public restrooms. "This is the last time," said John.

"Last time for what?" Kurt opened his door and got out.

"Last investigation."

"You realize you said that after both of our last two capers."

"This time I mean it."

Kurt chuckled. "You're hilarious."

"I'm not joking."

Kurt laughed some more as the two men walked along the concrete path that meandered through Jetty Park.

They crossed the street and walked up to the entrance. Kurt pulled open the door and John walked in.

Cole had the lights dimmed. Melvin Mulhern had gone home, but Kelly Morgan was sitting at the bar. A tall, thin man John and Kurt didn't know stood between two barstools. Cole stood across from him, looking down at some paperwork on the bar between them. An open briefcase sat on the bar to the unknown man's left. Cole glanced up when he heard John and Kurt walk in.

"Sign here and here," said the pale man, stabbing his index finger at the paperwork.

Cole looked back down and signed, and the man flipped to the next page.

"Here … and here," said the guy.

Cole signed again.

"Okay," the guy said. "That should do it." He laughed, as though he'd just said something funny.

Cole glared at the man.

"Hey, Cole," said Kurt.

Cole nodded.

John and Kurt sat down near Kelly.

"Who's that?" Kurt asked.

"I dunno," Kelly replied. "Some lawyer."

"Cole gettin' sued, or something?"

"I don't think so."

Cole laid his pen down on the bar. "Well, thanks, Marty," he said.

"Like I told ya," Marty said, "the right amount of cash and the right signatures can make anything happen."

"Yeah, yeah."

Marty closed his briefcase. "Any questions, just call."

"Yeah."

Marty turned and walked out the door.

"Who's that?" Kurt asked.

"Martin Gold," Cole replied. "He's a lawyer."

"*Your* lawyer?" John questioned.

"Fuck no," Cole shot back. "I wouldn't trust that shyster with …" He trailed off as he shuffled through the paperwork before him. He picked up an ID card and showed it to the guys. "What do you think?"

John leaned in for a closer look. "Cole Ballinger, Private Investigator," he read. "You just got that?"

"Yep."

"Congratulations."

"Thanks."

"Let me see that," said Kurt, holding out his hand.

Cole handed him the laminated identification card.

"Nice," Kurt said, as he inspected it. "I want one."

"You already have one," John mumbled.

"I mean a real one."

"What're you talking about?" Cole asked.

"Nothing," said Kurt.

Kelly Morgan slid his empty bottle of Bud Light across the bar. "Hit me," he ordered.

Cole turned to grab Kelly another beer out of the cooler. "Can I get you guys some menus?" he asked. He twisted off Kelly's cap and placed the bottle in front of him.

"Yep," Kurt said, "and we have some news on our case."

"On your case, huh?" Cole grabbed two menus off the back bar and tossed them in front of Kurt and John. "Let me guess ,Rosie the bartender dreamed one of the two of you were next."

John and Kurt looked at each other and back at Cole. "Don't even joke about that," said Kurt.

"A neighbor of Conner Cady's offered up some information this evening," John said.

"I'm listening," said Cole, "but not real well." He and Kelly chuckled.

"Mark Steuben and Vicky Cady were sleeping together," John said, "and Florence Ivy managed the hotel where they would meet."

"You're shittin' me," said Cole.

"I'm not shittin' you," John assured him.

"I did not see that coming."

"What should we do next?" Kurt asked.

Cole thought for a second. "Didn't you say Vicky Cady fell down the stairs at her home?"

"Yes."

"Where was her husband when it happened?"

"He was at work," John replied.

"Are you sure?"

"That's what Conner and the neighbor both said."

"Where was Mark Steuben's wife at the time?"

"We don't know, but she was jogging with Mark when he was hit by the car, so she didn't do it."

"Where was Conner Cady when Steuben was run over?"

John slowly nodded his head. "You think they killed each other's spouse."

"Just like in the Hitchcock film," said Kurt.

"*Throw Momma from the Train* was a Hitchcock film?" Kelly asked.

"No, *Strangers on a Train*," said John.

"With Danny DeVito?"

"No! *Throw Momma from the Train* was inspired by the Hitchcock film *Strangers on a Train*," said John. "A tennis player and a wacko meet on a train and decide to exchange murders so neither one of them get caught."

"Huh," said Kelly. "Was Billy Crystal the tennis player?"

John stared at Kelly in disbelief.

"Ha!" Kelly said, pointing at John. "I'm just bustin' your balls."

John returned his attention to Cole. "You think the two of them exchanged murders?" he asked.

Cole shrugged. "That's for you to find out."

"Should we call the police?" Kurt asked.

"I'd wait till I had more evidence," Cole responded.

"Like what?"

"Find out where each other's spouse was at the time of the murders."

"Gotcha. I'll just have an order of wings and an order of onion rings."

"You?" Cole asked John.

"I'll have the Cuban sandwich."

"I'll put those orders in."

"You gonna ask me if I want anything?" Kelly asked.

"You want something?"

"No, I already ate."

"When will I learn?"

Chapter Sixteen

Kurt showed up at John's place at eight o'clock on Thursday morning with a bag of McDonald's food and a cardboard tray containing three medium coffees. He knocked on the front door with his foot, but no one answered. He walked around to the rear sliding glass door and knocked on that; there was still no answer. He carried the bag and tray to a lounge chair and set it down on the plastic end table. He took out his cell phone, sat in the lounge and dialed John's number; it went straight to voicemail.

Kurt tossed his cell on the table next to the bag, opened the bag, and took out one of the three Hash Browns. He took a bite of the crispy potato patty and immediately sucked air into his mouth in an attempt to cool it.

Holy shit! he thought. *How is it still that hot?*

He picked up a cup of coffee, took off the lid, and blew into it.

Cassie's back door opened.

Kurt's head spun around.

"Hey, string bean!" Cassie hollered.

"Hey, Cassie," said Kurt. "You want a coffee? I brought an extra."

"Sounds great. Give me a sec."

Cassie pulled her head back inside and the screen door shut behind her.

Kurt sipped his coffee and checked John's slider several times as he waited for Cassie to return. When she finally did, she was dressed in gray yoga pants and a black tank top. She walked across the backyards and sat down on the lounge chair next to Kurt.

"I was just going to run to the store to pick up some coffee," said Cassie. "I'm all out."

"Looks like I saved the day."

"Looks like you did," Cassie picked up a cup and took off the lid. "There, that should be cool enough to drink in about an hour."

"Just don't spill it in your lap, in case you plan on having kids someday."

Cassie giggled. "Where's John?"

"I knocked. He didn't answer, and his cell went right to voicemail. There's a couple sandwiches in that bag. Help yourself."

"Don't mind if I do," she said, jamming her hand into the bag.

"Did you work last night?" Kurt asked.

"Yeah."

"Did you speak with Rosie?"

"She called in. Russel was pissed."

"She sick?"

"No. I guess she's got some knew boyfriend. A writer."

"Charlie Hewitt."

"Yeah, that's him. You know him?"

"I've met him."

"I'm gonna take the McGriddle. Is that okay?"

"Sure."

"Rosie said Charlie kicked the ever lovin' shit outta her ex." Cassie unwrapped the breakfast sandwich and pulled the cheese off the wrapper with her teeth.

"John and I were there when it happened."

"Oh, she didn't mention that."

"So, she just called in to spend time with him?"

"I guess. She said they were driving up to Orlando last night; Charlie had business up there, or something."

"Were they spending the night in Orlando?"

"I don't think so. Why?"

"No reason."

"Does Charlie seem like a nice guy?" Cassie asked.

"Yeah, I guess."

"That's good, because Abel was a jerk. Rosie's a nice girl. She deserves a nice guy."

"I guess." Kurt took another bite of his Hash Brown and washed it down with coffee. "Did Rosie tell you about the third victim?"

"No, she said we would talk Friday night."

"She's not working tonight either?"

"No. Tonight's her scheduled night off. What happened with the third victim?"

"The woman's name is, or was, Florence Ivy, a motel manager in Fort Pierce."

"What motel?"

"The Seagull Motel."

"I know that place."

"How do you know it?"

"I just know it. What happened to her?"

"She was shot in the head while walking from her car to the office."

"Yikes. That's awful."

"Here's the best part: the first victim—Vicky Cady—and the second victim—Mark Steuben—were having an affair."

"No kidding?"

"Damn straight. And their rendezvous was the Seagull Motel."

"Wow."

"Yeah."

"I gotta hand it to ya, Kurt," said Cassie, "that's some really great detective work."

Kurt nodded proudly. "Yeah, we're getting pretty good at crime-solving, if I do say so myself," he boasted, omitting the part about the neighbor who had told them everything they needed to know.

"Have you spoken with the police?"

"We ran what we know by Cole last night."

"The ex-cop who was here the other day."

"Yes. He said we should wait till we find out where Cady's husband was at the time of Steuben's hit-and-run, and where Steuben's wife was at the time of Cady's tumble down the stairs."

"So, Cole thinks they killed each the other's spouse."

"Pretty much."

"Just like in *Throw Momma from the Train*."

"Did you know that movie was based on an old Alfred Hitchcock movie?"

"Who?"

"Alfred—never mind. He was before my time, so he was way before your time." Kurt reached into the paper bag and pulled out a Breakfast Burrito, then he put his hand back in searching for packets of hot sauce. Feeling none, he tipped the bag toward him and looked inside. "Goddammit!"

"What's the matter?"

"No hot sauce. Stupid kids."

John's back door slid open. "My invitation must have gotten lost in the mail," he said.

John was wearing boxer shorts and carrying yesterday's T-shirt in his hand. He yawned big, and loud, and rubbed his eyes.

"I knocked on your door, and called your cell phone," said Kurt. "What were you doing in there?"

"Sleeping. It's only eight o'clock."

"I've been up since five," Kurt said. "You Hollywood types sleep too damn late."

"I haven't even gone to bed yet," Cassie offered.

"Are ya shittin' me?" Kurt asked.

"Nope. Left the club at three. Went to a house party in Stuart. Just got home a seven."

"And you still look amazing."

"Thanks, string bean."

John pulled his shirt over his head as he walked toward them.

"Coffee on the tray," said Kurt, "and a sandwich in the bag."

"Now that's service," John said. He picked up the last cup of coffee and removed the lid.

"I was just telling Kurt you guys did some really great detective work," Cassie said.

"On what?" John asked. He blew into his coffee and tested it with the tiniest of sips.

"Rosie's dream predictions. That was pretty awesome the way you pieced all the clues together to find out that the woman and the man were sleeping together at the Seagull Motel."

"Pieced what clues together?" John asked. "Cady's neighbor told us all about it."

Cassie shot Kurt a disappointed look.

Kurt shrugged.

"And to think I was so impressed with you, beanpole," said Cassie.

"Well, I mean, the neighbor did help us fill in a few of the gaps," said Kurt.

"The whole thing was a gap," John said. "So, yeah, I guess she did fill it in." He reached into the McDonald's bag. "What do ya got in here?" He pulled out a Hash Brown, held it between his teeth, and went back in for a sandwich.

"There's another burrito and a McMuffin of some sort," Kurt answered. "Take what you want."

John pulled out the burrito. "So, why *are* you here so early?" John asked.

"I figured you'd want to get started early and wrap this case up," Kurt replied.

"If wrap it up means call the police, then yes, I want to wrap it up."

"Call the police? I thought we were gonna see where the two spouses were at the time of the murders?"

"That's for the cops to figure out. The information we'll be giving them today is more than enough for them to open an investigation."

"But, I wanted to solve the case."

"We pretty much did."

Kurt sighed. "I guess."

"I think he's right Kurt," Cassie said. "Tell the cops what you know, and let them take it from there."

"And they'll take all the credit for our leg work."

"What leg work?" John asked. "The only leg work was walking next door to Cady's neighbor's house."

"What if there's another victim?" said Kurt.

"There won't be another victim," John assured him.

"Who should we give the information to—Spence Oller, Tommy Franklin, or Jack Helm?"

"I say we give it to Spence. After all, he was the one who got Ivy's name for us."

"Sounds good to me." Kurt reached back into the bag.

"What are you doing?" John asked.

Kurt pulled his empty hand out. "Getting the other sandwich."

"I thought it was mine?"

"You had a burrito."

"So did you."

"But a burrito isn't enough breakfast for me."

"Me neither."

"Christ, you two are just like children," said Cassie. She reached into the bag and yanked out the sandwich. "I'll settle it for you." She unwrapped the Egg McMuffin and took a big bite. "There, now it's mine."

"I'm gonna be starving in an hour," Kurt complained.

"Me too," said John.

"Not me," Cassie said. "I'm already stuffed."

"Second breakfast at Mulligan's?" Kurt asked.

"Sounds good to me," John responded. "Let me jump in the shower and we'll take off."

"Second breakfast," Cassie scoffed. "What's wrong with the two of you?"

Kurt chuckled. "Better women than you have asked that same—"

"Better woman than me?" Cassie asked.

"Yeah, I knew that was a stupid thing to say the minute it left my mouth."

Chapter Seventeen

After second breakfast at Mulligan's, John and Kurt hopped into Kurt's van and headed for the Breakwater Bar and Grill.

John reached into his pocket for his cell phone and dialed.

"Hey, Cole, it's John Burton."

"And what favor will you be asking for today?" Cole asked wearily.

John ignored the jab. "Are you at your bar?"

"I am."

"We're going to swing by."

"Swing away. Did you find out the whereabouts of the spouses?"

"No, but I think we've decided to hand the case over to the police."

"I think that's probably a good idea."

"We'd like to tell Spence everything we know, and let him take it from there. Is he there, by any chance?"

"No, but I'll give him a call."

"Thanks, Cole." John hung up his cell. "Cole's going to call Spence and have him meet us at the Breakwater."

"Uh-huh," Kurt responded.

"Are you mad at me?"

"No."

"You sound mad."

"I'm not. You think Spence will let us be there when they make the arrests?"

"Probably not."

Kurt sighed.

"I'm sure Spence will see that we get some of the credit for this," said John.

"I guess. But ya know, it would have been a lot better if we had learned the truth about Mark Steuben and Vicky Cady a few days earlier. It would have saved Florence Ivy's life."

"Yeah, I was trying not to think about that."

"I wonder how long Conner knew about the affair, and how long he waited to tell Steuben's wife?"

"Hard to say, but I'm sure Spence will keep us posted. He seems like a good guy."

"I guess."

Kurt made a right hand turn off of US 1 onto Seaway Drive, and headed over the Fort Pierce South Bridge. The runners and walkers crossing the bridge were taking advantage of the beautiful morning. The old Volkswagen micro bus began its descent on the east side of the bridge and Kurt brought it to a halt in front of Cole's bar.

"Not often we get a parking space right out front," said John.

"First time for everything," Kurt replied.

As John opened his door, the squeaky hinge caused a seagull that had been feasting on a discarded donut to fly away. As it flapped its wings the bird cried out in anger over the disruption of its breakfast.

"Winged rats," Kurt commented as the two men walked up to the entrance.

John wiped his forehead with the back of his hand. "Hot already," he said.

Kurt tugged on the door handle; it didn't budge.

"Locked," said Kurt.

"Knock," John said.

Just as Kurt lifted his fist to pound on the glass door, Leon, Cole's cook, yanked it open. His biceps looked like two black veiny pythons trying their best to escape the confines of his skin-tight, white T-shirt. Kurt flinched when Leon reached up to scratch his sweat-covered bald head.

"Whatever it is you be sellin', we ain't buyin'," said Leon in his silky-smooth baritone. He stood staring stone-faced at the two men.

Kurt shook his head. "We're not salesmen. I'm Kurt, and this is John Burton. We're friends of Cole's."

"I know who you are," Leon shot back. "That was what some uh you white folks call *jokin' around.*"

"We usually grin a little when we joke around," said Kurt.

"My humor's what they call black humor."

John snorted. "I get it."

"Get what?" Leon asked.

"Nothing."

"Is Cole here?" Kurt asked.

"He is. Come on in, guys."

"Thanks," Kurt said, as he turned sideways to squeeze past Leon.

The muscular cook made John squeeze past him as well before closing the door and turning around. "Boss!" he shouted.

Kurt flinched again.

"Christ, you a jumpy mother fucker, ain'tcha?" said Leon.

"Not usually," said Kurt.

Cole pushed through the kitchen's swinging door and walked into the bar. "I called Spence," he said. "He should be here in a bit."

"Thanks," said John.

"You had coffee yet?" Cole asked.

"Three cups already."

"I'll take a cup," said Kurt.

"Leon, can you grab a cup of coffee for Kurt?" Cole asked.

Leon was halfway to the kitchen. "He can get it himself. He's a big boy—a big, skinny, pale, gawky, gangly, lanky, boy." He pushed open the kitchen door and disappeared into the kitchen.

"Gangly and lanky are pretty much the same thing," Kurt mumbled.

"What's that?" Leon growled from the kitchen.

"Nothing!" Kurt shouted.

John's eyes widened. "Damn, he's got some good hearing," he whispered.

Cole stared at the kitchen door. "He's got good just about everything," he replied. "Sometimes I think he was created in a laboratory somewhere, like in that Dolph Lungren movie."

"*Universal Soldier*," Kurt offered.

"That's the one."

The entrance door opened, and all three men spun around. It was Detective Spence Oller.

"Hey, kid," said Cole.

"What's going on, guys?" Spence asked.

"Your friends wanted to talk to you about their case."

"The lady who dreams about murders?" Spence asked.

"That's the one," said Kurt.

"You need me to make another call for you?" Spence asked eagerly.

"We want you to call the police."

"I am the police," Spence said.

"We want you to take over from here," John said.

"Take over what exactly?"

"We learned from Conner Cady's neighbor that his wife was having an affair with Mark Steuben."

"Cady is the guy whose wife fell down the stairs?"

"Yes."

"And Mark Steuben was killed in the hit-and-run?"

"Yeah."

"Okay, that sounds like more than a coincidence."

"That's what we thought," said Kurt. "We're thinking they killed each other's spouse."

"Like in *Strangers on a Train*," said Spence, nodding his head. "What about the murder that took place here in Fort Pierce—the motel manager? How does she fit in?"

"Vicky Cady and Mark Steuben were meeting at the Seagull Motel," John replied.

"Huh. So … who killed her?"

"We don't know," said John.

"But probably one of them," Kurt said.

"Why would they kill her?"

"To tie up loose ends maybe. I don't know."

"It's enough to bring them in for questioning, isn't it?" John asked.

"More than enough," Spence answered.

"So, you can take it from here?" John asked.

"I can." Spence looked to Cole, who was now behind the bar with his back to them. Arms folded across his chest; he was staring out the window over Jetty Park.

"I don't want to step on any toes," said Spence. "I'll have to let Tommy Franklin know what you've told me. The Florence Ivy homicide is his."

"Good idea," said Cole. "You don't want Tommy pissed at ya."

Spence pulled a notepad and pen out of the vest pocket of his sport jacket. "What did you say the name of your client was?"

"We didn't," said Kurt.

"I'll need to question her as well. So, I'll need her name."

"Her name is Rosie Barlow," John said.

Spence jotted it down. "Address?"

"Four-thirty California Avenue, in Stuart."

"You need the addresses for Steuben and Cady?" Kurt asked.

"Yes."

"I'll have to run out to my van and grab them." While Kurt did so, John asked Spence: "Could you hold off for a bit before speaking with Rosie? I'd like to drive over to her place and let her know what's going on before you just show up."

"Sure, John, but I'll want to speak with her first, so can you do it this morning?"

"Yeah."

"And I'll need Cady's neighbor's name and address."

"Kurt has it written down with the others."

"Good."

Kurt walked back through the door holding a few pieces of paper he'd ripped off of larger pieces to make his notes. "Here they are," he said, handing Spence the wad of papers.

"That's a great filing system ya got there, Kurt," Cole pointed out.

"Yeah, I need a cardboard box or something to put them in."

"That's what you need—a cardboard box," Cole responded.

"Let's go," John said.

"You're going over to speak with Rosie now?" Spence asked.

"Yes."

"Why are we going over there?" Kurt asked.

"Just to let her know what's going on, and to give her a heads up that Spence and Franklin will be speaking with her today."

"Good idea," said Kurt.

The two men told Spence and Cole goodbye and headed out the door. A seagull was noshing the moldy donut. John wondered if it was the same seagull. Probably not.

Kurt kicked at the gull. "Damn flyin' shit factories."

The two men climbed into Kurt's van and off they went.

As Kurt steered the van around Jetty Park, he said, "I never heard *Universal Soldier* described as a Dolph Lungren movie. I've always thought of it more as a Jean-Claude Van Damme movie."

"Yeah, I wondered about that myself."

"Kinda like calling *Tango and Cash* a Kurt Russell movie."

"Or more like calling *Tarzan the Ape Man* a Maureen O'Sullivan movie."

"Although I do consider the other *Tarzan the Ape Man* a Bo Derek movie."

"Bo Derek," the men whispered in unison as they gazed out the front windshield, remembering the posters that had hung on their bedroom walls.

Chapter Eighteen

Kurt shoved the shifter into park and shut off the engine across the street from Rosie's apartment on California Avenue.

"That same Porsche was parked here the other day," said John. "You think that's Rosie's car? How much do you think a bartender at a gentlemen's club makes?"

"I can't imagine it would be enough to afford that car. Looks like a 2018 or thereabouts?"

John gave the door handle a pull. "Yeah, looks pretty new."

The two men crossed the street and walked up the stairs to the second floor. Kurt gave the door a rap.

"She went to Orlando yesterday with the writer," said Kurt, disgustedly.

"What's wrong with that?" John asked.

"What's she see in that guy?" Kurt knocked again.

"He's good-looking, he's in good shape, he's tough, he's an artist, he's closer to her age than you are, he's—"

"Why don't you marry him, John. *Sheesh.*"

Rosie pulled open the door. She was wearing a robe and holding it closed with her fist. "Hey, guys," she said. "What's up?"

"Are we interrupting something?" John asked.

Rosie smiled. "Nope."

"Can we speak to you for a second?"

"Of course."

Rosie stepped back to let them enter. She closed the door behind them and tied her belt around her waist. "I haven't had any more dreams, if that's what you're wondering."

"No," said Kurt. He craned his neck toward the bedroom door. "Someone else here?"

"Charlie."

"Oh."

"We just wanted to let you know that a couple detectives from Fort Pierce would be stopping by here today to speak with you," said John.

"About my dreams?"

"More or less," said Kurt.

"Kurt and I made the connections between the three victims. The third one was murdered, and we believe the first two were as well."

"Oh my gosh."

"Who is it, babe?" said Charlie, walking from the bedroom into the living room wearing only jeans and loafers and carrying a black T-shirt. "Oh, hey guys." Charlie approached the two men smiling, with his hand extended. "How's it going?"

Kurt, jealously noting Charlie's chiseled physique, shook his hand half-heartedly. He was relieved when Charlie slipped the shirt over his torso.

"Good, Charlie," John said, also shaking. "Just stopped by to touch base with Rosie."

"About her dreams?"

"Yep."

Charlie grinned at Rosie, then returned his gaze to John. "The dreams seem to be over with."

"I hope so."

"We just wanted to let her know that a couple of detectives from Fort Pierce would be around later today to speak with her," said Kurt.

"Oh yeah?" said Charlie. "Why's that?"

"We think all three of the people she dreamed about were murdered."

"Ya don't say."

"Yeah," John added, "We think the one woman's husband killed the other woman's husband, and vice versa."

"Why?" Charlie asked.

"We found out from a neighbor that the spouses were having an affair."

"No kidding! What about the third woman?"

"She owned the motel where the two would meet."

"Wow, that's crazy."

"Might be a good storyline for one of your books," said John.

Kurt shot his buddy a look. "Or one of our screenplays."

Charlie chuckled and put up his hands. "Don't worry, Kurt, I won't use it." He reached for his cell phone and checked the screen. "You guys will have to excuse me. I gotta take this. It's my editor."

"You can take it in the bedroom, hon," said Rosie.

"Thanks, babe, but there's some paperwork I need to look at downstairs while I'm talking to him." Charlie tapped the screen and put the cell phone to his ear. "Hey, what's up?" he asked, on the way out the door.

"Sit down, guys," said Rosie. "Can I get you a cup of coffee?"

"No, thanks, I've—"

"I'll have a cup," said Kurt. "But first, can I use your bathroom?"

"Sure," said Rosie, pointing. "Right through that door. Ya gotta go through my bedroom to get to the bathroom."

"Thanks."

Kurt walked toward the bedroom and John took a seat on the sofa, as Rosie grabbed a mug out of the cabinet.

"Are the detectives coming soon?" Rosie asked. "Charlie's taking me to lunch, and then we're going to the beach."

"Spence said he wanted to speak with you first, so I would imagine they'll be right along."

"Spence is one of the detectives?"

"Yes."

"Is he a friend of yours?"

"A friend of a friend."

Rosie poured the coffee into the mug. "Does Kurt like milk or sugar?"

"Neither."

Rosie walked to the table and set down the mug.

"You and Charlie seem to be getting along really well," said John.

"Oh, he's wonderful," said Rosie. "I want him to meet my parents, but I know it's way too soon."

"I would think so."

"He's so smart, and so nice to me."

"A big change from Abel."

"Ain't that the truth."

Kurt stepped into the doorway and stared at John.

"Coffee's on the table," John informed him, pointing.

Kurt said nothing. His eyes went to Rosie.

"What's the matter with you?" John asked.

Rosie turned around to face Kurt. "Is everything okay? Just jiggle the handle if it keeps running."

"John, can you step into the bedroom with me for a second?" Kurt asked.

"Only if you buy me dinner," John joked.

Rosie giggled.

"Now, John."

John cocked his head. "What are you—"

"Right now."

John stood and walked to the bedroom door. Rosie stayed where she was. Kurt turned and pointed to a heat vent in the bedroom floor. John started to say something, but Kurt put his finger to his lips to shush him.

"The vent," Kurt whispered. "Listen."

John walked to the vent with Kurt. Kurt knelt down, pulling John's T-shirt with him. John got down on his hands and knees. He could hear a voice coming from the vent.

"Listen," Kurt whispered again.

The two men put their ears to the vent.

"You don't have anything to worry about," came a man's voice from the vent.

"It's Charlie," John whispered.

Rosie was now standing in the doorway.

"What are you guys doing?" she asked.

"*Shhh,*" said Kurt.

"You weren't home when your wife had her accident," said Charlie, "and Steuben's wife was with him when *his* accident occurred. You both have alibis."

There was silence for a few seconds, and then Charlie said, "Your wife and Steuben never signed a guest book, or even paid for a room for that matter. Ivy was an acquaintance of your wife's—she let her use the motel room for free. She probably never told anyone. The place has no exterior security cameras. There's no need to panic. It comes down to the word of a neighbor that any good attorney could discredit."

There was more silence. Rosie walked to the vent and lowered herself. All three of them had their ears to the vent.

"When the detectives show up, just answer their questions. And make sure you don't mention my name, Cady, or you'll be victim number four. I've been doing this a long time. My name comes up, and there'll be no place for you to hide. You also better give Steuben a call and let her know I'm not fuckin' around."

The silence was a little longer than usual this time.

"What do you think he's doing?" Kurt asked.

"I don't know," John replied.

"He killed those people," Rosie whispered. "I can't believe it. I didn't dream it. I heard it at night through the vent."

"Looks that way," said Kurt.

"Shhh," said John. He put his ear closer to the vent.

Rosie moaned. "I was going to introduce him to my mom and dad."

"I think that would be a big mistake," said Kurt. "I knew there was something I didn't like about that guy."

"He was so nice," Rosie said.

"Well, not to everyone," Kurt said.

"We better call Spence," John said, taking his cell phone out of the side pocket of his cargo shorts.

"No, I don't think you better," said Charlie.

The trio's heads snapped around. They all froze when they saw Charlie standing in the doorway, his SIG Sauer P226 trained on them. He held the semi-automatic in his right hand, about waist high.

"Get up," Charlie ordered. He sidestepped to the bed and grabbed a small red and white checkered throw pillow with his left hand. "Drop the cell phone."

John did as he was told. The cell bounced on the carpeting and came to rest face up at his knees.

"Either one of you have a weapon?" Charlie asked.

"Not on me," said Kurt.

John shook his head.

"On your feet," said Charlie.

They slowly got to their feet.

"You don't have to do this," John said.

Charlie snorted. "Of course I do," he said. He sidestepped to the doorway and backed through. "Come on, into the living room."

"No, you don't," John continued. "You kill us, the cops are coming after you. You let us live, they're still coming after you. You don't have to kill us."

Charlie pursed his lips and stared at John in thought.

"Someone will hear the gunshots," said Kurt.

"The pillow will muffle them enough. When questioned, the neighbors will just say they thought they heard an odd sound."

Rosie sniffed. A single tear rolled down her check. She sniffed again. Her hands were trembling.

"I really liked you," said Rosie. Her voice was shaky.

"I liked you too, babe, but it never would have worked. I mean, a bartender and a hitman? Come on."

"I thought you were a writer," said Rosie.

"Naw, babe, I have a ghostwriter I pay to write that crap. Sure, I mean, every once in a while I come up with an idea, but I don't do the writing."

"It's just a cover," said Kurt. "Book series that take place around the country. You just say you're there doing research."

"Just like you did here," John added. "Perfect cover."

"It *was* the perfect cover, till you two screwed it up. Now I gotta lay low for a while and come up with something else. I think that's why I'm gonna shoot you, just because you frigged up my life."

"Rosie didn't do anything," Kurt protested. "Let *her* go."

Charlie sighed. He thought for a second. "Yeah, okay." He looked at Rosie. "Babe, I want you to go in the bathroom and shut the door. Get in the shower, close the door, and put your fingers in your ears real tight like, so you don't have to hear the Hardy Boys here go bye-bye."

Rosie looked from John to Kurt.

John nodded. "Go ahead, Rosie," he said. "It's gonna be okay."

Rosie moved slowly toward the bedroom door.

"Oh, and Rosie," John said, "tell my parents I love them … and tell Jessica I love her too."

"Yeah," Kurt said, "tell my mom and dad I love them too."

Charlie dropped the gun to his side. "Aw, come on guys. I can't do this. I'm not a monster."

"You kill people for a living," said Kurt.

"Shut up, Kurt," John said.

"I kill people for money, and I kill people I hate," said Charlie. "I don't kill my friends."

"Yeah," Kurt said, "we're your friends."

"I know," Charlie groaned. "I don't usually make friends this fast. I mean, I think I'm a likable guy."

"You are," said Kurt, nodding feverishly. "You're very likable. I like you. John likes you."

"Thanks, Kurt."

"Who paid you to kill Mark Steuben and Vicky Cady?" John asked.

"Their spouses got together and split my fee. I gave them a little discount too—three for the price of one. I know what cheating does to a family. My dad was a real dick to my mom until … "

"Until you killed him?" Kurt surmised.

"Christ, no! I didn't kill him; he was my dad, for shit's sake. He had a massive heart attack on Thanksgiving. Went face-first into his mashed potatoes and gravy. Poor guy never knew what hit him. Worst Thanksgiving of my life."

"I can imagine," said John.

"Okay, listen," said Charlie. "If I let all of you live, do you promise not to call the cops for at least an hour?"

They all nodded their heads.

"Ya gotta say it."

"Yes," they all said.

"You have to promise."

At the same time, all three of them nodded their heads and said, "We promise."

"Okay. It was really nice meeting you guys. I hope we see each other again sometime."

Charlie turned and hurried to the door. He slammed the door behind him, and ran down the stairs.

Kurt walked to the front window and looked out. "The Porsche is his," he said. He watched as Charlie jumped into the driver's seat, started the car, and sped off down the street.

"Well," said Kurt, "I guess we better call the police."

"But we promised," said Rosie.

"Because he had a gun," Kurt said.

"I'm not calling the cops," John said.

"Why not?" Kurt asked.

"Because he might get away anyway, and then he might come back some day, and the next time we see him, he might not be so friendly."

Kurt looked through the bedroom door at John's cell phone lying on the floor. "You might have a point there, buddy."

"But if we don't call the police," said John, "he goes on to kill more people."

"So, what do you want to do?" Kurt asked.

"I say we let him go," Rosie replied.

"Yeah, because you had the hots for him," Kurt shot back.

"So?" said Rosie.

"So?" Kurt aped.

"Maybe we better phone Spence," said John.

"It's your call," Kurt responded. "I'll do whatever you think."

"Grab my cell phone."

Kurt hurried to the cell, picked it up, and tossed it to John.

"Do you have his number?" Kurt asked.

"No."

"Call Cole."

John dialed.

"Hey, the killer was a hitman," he said, skipping the pleasantries. "Conner Cady and Margie Steuben paid him to kill their spouses, and Florence Ivy."

"How do you know this?"

"He told us. Rosie wasn't dreaming about the murders," John explained. "She heard Charlie through the heat vent."

"Who's Charlie?"

"The hitman. He lived downstairs from Rosie. She heard him through the vent talking about the murders."

"You shittin' me?"

"No. Can you tell Spence to meet us at Rosie's as quick as he can?"

"Where's this Charlie guy now?"

"He left."

"Left? Is he coming back?"

"Well, no. Can you please call Spence?"

"I'll call him and have him call you."

"Thanks, Cole." John hung up his cell phone and slipped it into his pocket. "Spence is gonna call me."

"Looks like this might take an hour after all," said Kurt.

John looked over at Rosie, who was now staring out the front window. "Oh, and, Rosie," he said.

"Yeah, John?"

"That thing I told you to tell Jessica … that stays in this room."

"So, don't tell her?"

"No."

"Okay." Rosie returned her attention to the street out front. "You think I'll ever see him again?" she asked.

"Let's hope not," Kurt replied.

"That's not very nice, Kurt. Why would you say that?"

"Because he's an assassin, Rosie."

"But he doesn't kill his friends."

"Oh, yeah, I forgot." Kurt shook his head. "Maybe he will come back. You can introduce him to your folks. Mom, Dad, this is Charlie Hewitt. He's a hitman. He kills people for a living, but not his friends. Maybe the two of you can get married, settle down, and have little hit-children of your own. Your little girl will just love Take Your Daughter to Work Day."

Rosie smiled. "That would be nice, Kurt. Thanks; I feel better now."

"Good grief."

Chapter Nineteen

Four nights later, John and Kurt were relaxing poolside. They both wore board shorts. Kurt was shirtless and John was wearing a white T-shirt with the *Law of the Land* logo on the front. Two bottles of LandShark Lager sat on the table between them. On the cement to John's left was his old Coleman ice chest.

"I'd really like one of those T-shirts," said Kurt. "Ya got any more?"

"There's two boxes of them at my parents' house," John replied. "Next time we're over there, remind me, and I'll get you a couple."

"I guess I better get one for Sara too. If I show up at work wearing one, she'll wonder where her's is."

"What are the chances you'll show up at work though?"

"I guess you're right." Kurt chuckled. "You hear anything from Spence or Cole?"

"Not since Friday when we were questioned."

"I haven't seen anything on the news about any arrests made."

"Me neither." John picked up his beer and sipped it.

Just then Cole and Spence walked around the corner of the house.

"Shit, it's the fuzz," said Kurt.

John chuckled.

Cole was dressed in a black T-shirt and jean shorts. Spence was still wearing his light gray suit from work.

"What's up, guys?" said Cole.

Kurt lifted his beer. "Not much, boys," he replied. "Nice jorts, Cole."

Cole shook his head. "Trista bought them for me."

"Was she pissed at ya?" John asked.

"You think I haven't heard that one already?"

"And yet you wore them again anyway."

Cole looked down and inspected the shorts. "I really don't think they look that bad."

"What's your seein' eye dog think?" Kurt joshed.

Spence and Kurt laughed.

"Okay, shut up," said Cole, "and hand me one of those beers."

John lifted the Coleman's lid and handed Cole a bottle as he headed for one of the empty lounge chairs.

"Thanks," said Cole.

Spence stood near the edge of the pool.

"Beer, Spence?" John asked.

"No, I can't. I gotta get going in a minute. I just stopped by to touch base. We arrested Margie Steuben and Conner Cady this morning for solicitation of murder for hire and conspiracy—both first degree felony charges."

"Any word on Charlie Hewitt?" John asked.

"Nothing. His Porsche was discovered abandoned and burned by Ocala PD Saturday morning. I doubt his real name was Charlie Hewitt, but we've issued a BOLO on him, and we're circulating the photo from his Amazon book page."

"He told us it was a ghost writer who wrote his books," said Kurt. "Anything on that? I mean, he must have had a bank account, social security number, things like that."

"He did have a small checking account that money from his book sales was direct deposited into, but there hasn't been any activity on it since someone switched the direct deposits from that account to Rosie Barlow's checking account."

Kurt did a spit take. "Rosie's account!" he sputtered. "You mean the sales from his books are going to her?"

Spence nodded. "Yes."

"Is that even legal?"

"Charlie can't legally profit off any of his crimes, but the books are works of fiction, and we don't know what past crimes he's committed. The DA is checking into it, but so far it's all legal."

"Wow," said John, "maybe Charlie really did like Rosie."

"Or maybe he's still in contact with her," said Cole.

"What's she say about it?" Kurt asked.

"She claims to have no idea why Hewitt would do such a thing," said Spence, "and says she's had no contact with him."

"You believe her?"

"We have no reason not to, but we'll keep an eye on her."

"One more thing," Kurt said. "Did you mention that John and I assisted in the investigation?"

"Yes, Kurt."

"Thanks, buddy. You think it'll be in the newspaper?"

"I'm sure it will."

"Awesome."

"Well, I better get going," Spence said. "I have to pick up Allison at eight."

"Take it easy, Spence," John said.

Spence turned and walked back the way he came.

Kurt looked to Cole. "Aren't you riding with him?" he asked.

"Nope," Cole replied.

"Did you drive separately?"

"Nope."

"How are you getting back to the bar?"

"One of you two can drive me back after I've had a couple beers."

"But I was going—"

"I'll buy you dinner."

"You got yourself a deal, pal."

The End

Coming Soon:

The Maine Events

From the Tales of Dan Coast

A Note From the Grave

ALSO BY RODNEY RIESEL

From the Tales of Dan Coast Series

Sleeping Dogs Lie
Ocean Floors
The Coast of Christmas Past
Ship of Fools
Double Trouble
Most Likely to Die
Deadly Moves
On the Wagon
No Enemies Here
Neighborhood Watch
Another Mother
Corner Office
What He Doesn't Know
Shoulda Seen it Comin'

Jake Stellar Series

North Murder Beach
Beach Shoot
When Death Returns
The Obedience of Fools
Dead in the Water
Excited About Nothing
Southern Exposure

The Dunquin Cove Series

The Man in Room Number Four
Return to Dunquin Cove
Local Hero

Sunrise City Series

Sunrise City

Sunrise City 2: From Bad to Worse

Sunrise City 3: Never Strikes Twice

Sunrise City 4: Dig Two Graves

Sunrise City 5: Scapegoats

Fernandina Beach Mysteries

Maintenance Required

High Maintenance

Serial Maintenance

Family Maintenance

Jensen Beach Mysteries

As Seen on TV

TV or Not TV

From Here to There: A Collection of Short Stories